PENGUIN CANADA

VINYL CAFE UNPLUGGED

Master storyteller and humorist STUART McLEAN writes and hosts the popular CBC Radio show *The Vinyl Cafe*. He is the author of the bestselling books *Vinyl Cafe Diaries*, which won the short fiction award from the Canadian Authors Association; *Home from the Vinyl Cafe*, which won the Stephen Leacock Award for Humour; and *Welcome Home: Travels in Smalltown Canada,* which was awarded the CAA's prize for non-fiction.

ALSO BY STUART McLEAN

STUART McLEAN

VINYL CAFE
Unplugged

PENGUIN
CANADA

PENGUIN CANADA

Published by the Penguin Group

Penguin Group (Canada), 90 Eglinton Avenue East, Suite 700, Toronto, Ontario, Canada M4P 2Y3
(a division of Pearson Canada Inc.)

Penguin Group (USA) Inc., 375 Hudson Street, New York, New York 10014, U.S.A.
Penguin Books Ltd, 80 Strand, London WC2R 0RL, England
Penguin Ireland, 25 St Stephen's Green, Dublin 2, Ireland (a division of Penguin Books Ltd)
Penguin Group (Australia), 250 Camberwell Road, Camberwell, Victoria 3124, Australia
(a division of Pearson Australia Group Pty Ltd)
Penguin Books India Pvt Ltd, 11 Community Centre, Panchsheel Park, New Delhi – 110 017, India
Penguin Group (NZ), cnr Airborne and Rosedale Roads, Albany, Auckland 1310, New Zealand
(a division of Pearson New Zealand Ltd)
Penguin Books (South Africa) (Pty) Ltd, 24 Sturdee Avenue, Rosebank, Johannesburg 2196, South Africa

Penguin Books Ltd, Registered Offices: 80 Strand, London WC2R 0RL, England

First published in Viking Canada hardcover by Penguin Group (Canada),
a division of Pearson Canada Inc., 2000
Published in Penguin Canada paperback by Penguin Group (Canada),
a division of Pearson Canada Inc., 2001
Published in this edition, 2006

1 2 3 4 5 6 7 8 9 10 (OPM)

Copyright © Stuart McLean, 2000

LIBRARY AND ARCHIVES CANADA CATALOGUING IN PUBLICATION

McLean, Stuart, 1948–
Vinyl cafe unplugged / Stuart McLean.

First published: Toronto : Viking, 2000.
ISBN-13: 978-0-14-305216-6
ISBN-10: 0-14-305216-0

I. Title.

PS8575.L448V56   2006   C813'.54   C2006-904913-0

Visit the Penguin Group (Canada) website at **www.penguin.ca**

Visit *The Vinyl Cafe* website at **www.cbc.ca/vinylcafe**

Special and corporate bulk purchase rates available; please see
www.penguin.ca/corporatesales or call 1-800-399-6858, ext. 477 or 474.

For David Amer, who said one day,
"We should do a radio show together."

Mix a little folly with your plans:
It is sweet to be silly at the right moment.

HORACE, 65–8 B.C.

Contents

PET SOUNDS

Arthur

At five in the morning, on a sticky Tuesday in July, Dave woke up sweating. He reached out with his foot and wasn't surprised to discover he was alone in bed. He found Morley downstairs, sitting at the kitchen table. She was reading the paper.

"I was hot," she said.

"Me too," said Dave, flopping into a chair.

It was cool downstairs. It was cool everywhere in the house except for their bedroom.

"I don't get it," said Dave. "I'll call that guy again."

The air-conditioner guy came after lunch. He knelt by the vent in the floor of their bedroom.

"It's working," he said accusingly.

He was there for five minutes. For this he charged fifty dollars.

But he was right. When you held your hand over the vent, you could feel the cool air. Yet every night they woke up hot.

This was the second time in less than a year that Dave had called a repairman to examine the bedroom vent. They had a guy come in the winter too. In February Dave and Morley kept waking up cold.

In February when the furnace guy came, he held *his* hand over the vent and said, "Hot air," as if they were crazy. And then, because Dave insisted, he vacuumed the vent. Half an hour, seventy-five dollars. And still all winter they kept waking up freezing. And now it was summer and they were waking up hot.

It was Sam who figured it out. One night Dave found Sam sitting on the vent in their bedroom.

"What are you doing?" asked Dave.

"It feels good," said Sam. "The cool air. It's where Arthur sleeps."

Arthur the dog.

Arthur the sleeping machine.

Arthur the plug.

"Jesus," said Dave.

When he was a puppy, Arthur was allowed to sleep on Dave and Morley's bed. When he got bigger, they tried to move him to the floor and found they had a battle on their hands. They found that no dog in the world was more determined or skilled at insinuating himself onto a bed than Arthur.

They bought him a basket and put it in the hall. Arthur would make a big deal of climbing into his basket every night—circling it neurotically, sighing and grunting as he worried his blanket into a pleasing hump. But as soon as Dave and Morley were breathing rhythmically, Arthur's head would rise like a periscope and he would slide over the edge of his basket and work his way into the bedroom, keeping low to the ground, as if he were hunting. He would stop a foot short of the bed and cock an ear. If he didn't like the way one of them was breathing, he would bring his face close to theirs and listen, sometimes for five or ten minutes, staring at them like a priest taking confession, his wet nose only six inches away.

One night Dave woke up when Arthur was in the middle of his reconnaissance. When Dave opened his eyes all he could see were two huge eyeballs glaring back at him. They were so close Dave couldn't tell these were Arthur's eyeballs he was looking into. All he could see were two black pupils surrounded by hair. He smelled the sour breath of death that seemed to belong to these eyes and he soared upright, waking Morley with his gasp and sending Arthur bounding to his basket. When Morley opened *her* eyes, Dave was standing on his pillow pointing at the door.

"The dog," he said.

Arthur was in his basket, snoring.

"You're having a dream," said Morley. "Lie down."

Dave didn't get back to sleep for hours.

If Arthur was satisfied Dave and Morley *were* asleep when he crept into their bedroom, he would lift one paw slowly onto the bed and place it there without moving another muscle. If neither of them stirred, the other paw would go up just as slowly. Then, like a mummy rising from a swamp, Arthur would pull his body onto the bed and settle near their feet with a sigh, taking at first as little space as possible, but slowly unfolding and expanding as the night wore on—as if he were being inflated. He liked to work his *body* between theirs on his *way* towards the pillows.

One night in a dream Dave saw himself sleeping on the floor, in the corner of his bedroom, like a child servant from the Middle Ages. He looked at the bed to see who his master was and Dave saw *Arthur*. Wearing *his* pyjamas. Lying in *his* spot. Arthur had one paw behind his head and the other resting gently on Morley's back. In the dream, when Dave tried to get back into bed, Arthur bared his teeth, snarled and drew Morley closer.

When Dave woke up, he was, in fact, in his bed, and not on the floor, but Arthur was lying beside him with his head on the pillow, snoring (it was Arthur's snores that had woken him). Morley had disappeared. Dave found her in Sam's bed.

The next night when Arthur came into the bedroom and stared at him suspiciously, Dave said, "Get lost," and Arthur sighed and slunk away

Now he was hogging the vent.

On the Saturday after Sam had solved the air-conditioning mystery, Dave picked up a *Reader's Digest* while he was waiting in line to pay for groceries. He noticed an article called "Is Your Dog Your Boss?"

There was a test.

The test was straightforward. Get down on all fours and stare at your dog. If you are dominant, your dog will turn away. If your dog stares back, it means he considers you to be an inferior member of the pack. Dave drove home. He threw the frozen food in the freezer. He called Arthur. He dropped to his knees.

The thing that makes bad news worse is when it comes unexpectedly. Arthur had always been, if not considerate, at least obedient. Arthur might have pushed the limits but, unlike Sam and Stephanie, he usually did as he was told.

When Dave stared at Arthur, he fully expected him to turn tail. He had harboured the possibility of a little staring match. What he hadn't considered was that his dog would stop wagging his tail, hold his gaze for a full minute and then curl his lip and begin to walk menacingly forward, growling.

"Arthur?" said Dave.

Before the alarming moment resolved, Morley walked into the kitchen and Dave looked up at her, or more to the point, away from Arthur.

Arthur lifted his snout, sniffed derisively and ambled away, leaving Dave squatting on all fours, looking pathetically back and forth between his wife and the disdainful rear end of the retreating dog.

"Wait a minute," he called after Arthur. "That wasn't fair. Come back here."

But Arthur wasn't coming back.

"Arthur!" barked Dave, as firmly as he could.

Arthur was already around the corner, out of sight.

"Dave," said Morley softly, "what's going on?"

"Nothing," he said, struggling to his feet.

The summer Dave was seven he brought a notice home from Cubs about an overnight hike to the trouting pond behind Macaulays' farm. Dave had never slept away from home before. The whole idea made him nervous. He told his mother he didn't want to go.

"It will be all right," she said. "You'll see."

The evening before the sleep-out his father took him for a walk. They ended up in front of Angus MacDonnell's Post Office & General Store.

"You should have some supplies. For tomorrow night," his father said. He handed Dave fifty cents.

Dave had never had so much money to spend on candy in his life. He bought two Jersey Milk chocolate bars, fifteen blackballs (three for a penny), five pieces of red licorice, a package of Thrills and a bag of pink candied popcorn.

He rolled the candy up in his sleeping bag as his father suggested. Knowing it was in there as he shouldered his bag on the laneway that twisted through the Macaulays' sugarbush and over the hill to the trouting pond was the only thing that gave him the strength to turn his back on his father and start the long hike away from home.

After supper—burnt hot dogs and Kool-Aid—Dave sneaked into the tent and unrolled his sleeping bag. He had his mind on licorice. He didn't notice Joey Talarico following him. Joey spotted the stash and told Gordy Beaman and Billy Mitchell, who were a grade ahead of them, and pretty soon there were seven kids crowded around the tent. Dave felt compelled to share his candy. He handed it out, piece by piece. When everyone had something, there was nothing left for him. Later, when he crawled into his sleeping bag, Dave found the gold foil wrapper from one of the Jersey Milk bars and he licked it, looking for traces of melted chocolate. He then fell asleep crying.

That was the same year Dave got his first-ever brand-new baseball. It was his Easter present. A round, white leather orb with red lace—a miraculously beautiful thing that was both soft and hard at the same time. He took it to school after the holiday weekend in a blue velvet Crown Royal bag.

When Jim McDevitt saw Dave pull the ball out, he carefully tucked *his* new ball back into his school bag.

"Nice ball," he said to Dave.

By the end of summer Dave's beautiful ball was a mushy, torn, grey lump. But Jim McDevitt's was in the same pristine condition it had been on the Tuesday after the Easter weekend.

"You should've looked after it better," said Jim one day at recess.

Perhaps if Dave had been a different sort of person he would have remembered Jim McDevitt and the candy-guzzling Cubs before accepting the job of road manager for a heavy-metal group called Thrasher. Thrasher was in the third month of a year-long Tour of the World! when Dave signed on. The fact that the position was open at that point should have told him something. He caught up with Thrasher in a hotel bar after a disastrous show in Evansville, Indiana, during which the sound man had hurled a bottle of Scotch at

the lead singer and punched the drummer's girlfriend—leaving her unconscious in the wings, while
he stormed around the arena yanking cables out of
speakers in the middle of Thrasher's set. By noon the
next day, on the bus and already halfway to
Minneapolis, Dave had begun to appreciate just how
irreparably dysfunctional the crazed enterprise was.
The bass guitarist wouldn't get on the tour bus and was
driving himself to the gigs. The drummer's girlfriend,
who had been retching in the can since they left
Evansville, had already been banned from a rival
band's tour by a road manager because of how badly
she had messed up *their* drummer with the drugs she
provided him. The keyboard player hated everyone,
especially the bass guitarist; and the lead singer was so
strung out it had taken them half an hour to talk him
out of the hotel elevator that morning.

It took Dave four months to straighten things out. By
the end of the summer Thrasher was more or less back
together. Dave, on the other hand, was spinning apart.

His success didn't go unnoticed. Whenever the tour
lurched through New York or L.A., executives from the
record company told Dave he was the best road
manager they had. They praised his resourcefulness,
and his diplomacy, and his ability to smooth out the
most cantankerous local promoter. Most of all, they
said, the band loved him.

Well, they should have. Dave was doing just about
everything for them—picking up their dry cleaning,
driving their dates home, preparing home-cooked

meals on a two-burner camping stove he had bought in an army surplus store in Flint, Michigan, lending them money and writing "Dear John" letters for them as the bus rocked through the night. He finally quit the tour in Durham, North Carolina, after his fifth visit to see the lead singer's mother, who was in hospital recovering from surgery. The singer said that the stress of visiting a hospital and spending time with his mother would be too much for him to bear.

Dave lasted eight months with Thrasher. When he left, he vowed that he would never allow himself to be taken advantage of again.

And here he was, a quarter of a century later. Apparently he hadn't learned a thing about protecting his self-interest. Whenever he took a stand, especially whenever he tried to take a stand with his own family, no one ever paid him any attention. And if that wasn't enough, he had just learned that the dog ranked himself higher than Dave in the family hierarchy.

The Saturday evening after Arthur had delivered that disturbing news, Morley said, "Who wants to go for ice cream?"

Sam said, "Yes!" And then he said, "Ice cream, Arthur?"

Now ice cream happens to be Arthur's most favourite thing in the world. When Arthur heard the words "ice cream," his backside began to twist towards his head, his tail started wagging furiously and he crab-walked across the kitchen to Sam—the picture of a dog in heaven.

Dave said, "Let's go to the Dutch place."

Sam said, "Ice cream, Arthur."

Arthur's eyes started to roll back in his head.

That's when Morley said, "Dave, Arthur doesn't like the Dutch place. They don't have soft ice cream there."

There was a pointed silence.

They went to the Dairy Queen. They took a bowl for Arthur's ice cream. Dave watched the dog snorting it down, ice cream all over his face.

"Don't you think this is kind of peculiar?" he said to Morley as they watched the dog eat.

She looked at him strangely. She didn't understand.

Later in the week when Dave came home from work, he dug out the baseball mitts and said, "Where's Sam?" He thought they could go to the park. He thought they could throw the ball before supper. Sam was in the yard. He had Arthur tied to his wagon, pulling it up and down the sidewalk.

"I'm busy," he said. "I don't want to play ball now." Arthur gave Dave a look that seemed to say, *Butt out, Buddy*.

The next night Dave said he would make French fries for dinner. But there were no potatoes.

"Check Arthur's basket," said Morley.

Dave said, "What?"

When he is left alone in the house, Arthur steals potatoes. Somehow—no one knows how he does this, because no one has ever seen him do it—he can paw open the cupboard door where the potatoes are kept.

Arthur doesn't eat the potatoes. He carries them across the kitchen, drops them in his basket and sits on them. There is something about the feeling of being near raw potatoes that Arthur likes.

The night he was trying to make the French fries, Dave found five potatoes in Arthur's basket.

"Five's enough," said Morley.

"You mean," said Dave incredulously, "that you use potatoes that Arthur has sat on? You're telling me I have eaten potatoes from the dog basket?"

The final straw came a week later, when Dave found the socks. He was looking for potatoes in Arthur's basket and uncovered a stash of socks instead—ten single unmatched socks stuffed under the blanket. Dave held up the socks in disbelief. It was like finding an elephant graveyard. He went through the socks one by one. Nine of them were his. He had already thrown their partners out.

He looked at Arthur in horror.

"YOU?!!?" he said.

Arthur as much as shrugged as he walked out of the room.

Sam thought it was funny.

Morley said Dave was overreacting.

Stephanie said, "Why don't you just buy new socks? What's the big deal?"

Dave said, "That is not the point. You are missing the point."

Maybe, if someone had taken his side, things would have turned out differently.

But no one took his side, and that night Dave worked out what Arthur was costing them. Food, vet bills, shots, boarding when they went away (except they never went away because they didn't want to leave Arthur), potatoes.

"You know what he has probably cost us in potatoes?" said Dave. He was sitting at the kitchen table with a calculator, a pencil and a pad of paper. Morley was on the phone and waved him quiet. When she hung up, Dave began again.

"Where's the cost benefit here?"

Sam and Stephanie were watching television.

"Shhh!" said Stephanie.

"No one wants to hear this, Dave," said Morley as she left the room, adding, over her shoulder, "Why don't you work out what *I* cost?"

Dave said, "This is not a healthy relationship."

Stephanie said, "That's for sure."

Dave said, "If you had a roommate who behaved like that dog, you'd call the police. Or a lawyer."

No one was paying attention.

That night when he and Morley were reading in bed, Dave put his magazine down and said, "Name me one useful thing Arthur can do."

Morley sighed and rested her book on her stomach. "He can shake hands."

Dave propped himself up on an elbow.

"Listen to me. You know what he is? He's a wolf. He's just a small evolutionary step away from a wolf. Are you telling me you want to live with a wolf who can shake hands?"

On the weekend Dave went to Canadian Tire and came back with a doghouse made of extruded plastic. It was the last one left, white with dark plastic wood trim in the style of a Swiss ski chalet.

On Sunday night, Arthur went out into the yard. Into the doghouse.

"It's where a *dog* belongs," said Dave, coming back inside, washing his hands.

Not Arthur. Not, where *Arthur* belongs. As if he didn't know Arthur's name. As if they hadn't lived together for five years.

Dinner was morose, cutlery rattling coldly on china—everyone eating silently while Arthur stood by the back door and whimpered.

"No one say a word," said Dave.

On Monday, Dave arrived home with a huge bag of beef bones. He threw one into the backyard and the rest into the freezer. Arthur fell onto his bone with wolfish delight.

"See," said Dave, to no one in particular.

But at dinner Arthur was back at the door.

Whimpering.

They were all was hunched over their plates. No one wanted to make eye contact with Arthur. No one wanted to look at Dave.

Sam was pushing his food around his plate half-heartedly. When he reached for the milk jug to refill his glass for the third time, Morley stopped him and said, "Eat your fish first, Sam."

Sam said, "I hate fish."

Morley furrowed her brow. "You don't hate fish," she said.

Stephanie snorted, "He usually feeds his fish to Arthur."

Sam hit Stephanie.

Dave smiled triumphantly.

Tuesday night at supper when Arthur appeared at the back door, he was holding his paw up to his chest. He looked like a beggar.

Morley said, "He looks pathetic. He looks like he has been beaten up."

Dave shook his head. "He's faking. Don't pay any attention."

Arthur turned and limped back to his doghouse.

Dave said, "I'm not falling for that."

Supper was turning into an ordeal.

On Wednesday Dave said, "He's just trying to get our sympathy."

Sam stood up abruptly. "I can't stand this," he said. "I hate sausage." And he left the table.

Morley looked puzzled as she watched Sam storm off. "He has always liked sausage before."

Dave reached over to Sam's plate with his fork, speared one of the sausages and brought it over to his plate. "People used to believe that early man domesticated dogs." He pointed at his son's plate to see if anyone else wanted anything. "You know what they believe now? They believe that wolves took a look at human campfires and garbage piles and they recognized a good thing. They figured out ways of getting close to the fire without being eaten. They started to wag their tails and whimper—just like Arthur. These are just innate behaviours that have served them on their climb up the evolutionary ladder—behaviours that have helped them mooch off us."

He had Sam's last sausage on his fork. He was waving it between his wife and daughter. "Are you sure you don't want this?"

Morley stood up and walked away. She was going upstairs to talk to Sam.

"I'm serious," said Dave, raising his voice as she disappeared. "You don't have to be a brain surgeon to figure out it's better to curl up by a fire than fight it out in the wild. This is the latest research. We're being exploited by a wolf!"

"Arthur?" said Stephanie, who was the only one left at the table. "You're nuts."

"Theoretically," said Dave, "Arthur could turn on us at any time. He could drive us out of the cave."

On Thursday night when Dave took Arthur for his walk, the limp was more pronounced.

On Friday, after a block, Arthur sat down and wouldn't budge. Dave had to carry him home.

"Maybe," he said, "I should take him to the vet."

It was eleven-thirty at night.

"There's an all-night place," said Morley. "I took the guinea pig there once. Please call me if it's serious."

As he was heading out the door, Stephanie came downstairs with Arthur's blanket. She handed it to her father. "If you put him to sleep, I'm leaving home."

When Dave arrived at the clinic, there were two people in the waiting room. One of them, a young man with green spiked hair and a black leather jacket, was sitting stiffly in his seat holding a small cardboard box. Every few minutes there was a scuffling from the box and it jerked about in his lap. The other person, a man in a charcoal suit, was slumped back and staring at the ceiling. He looked like someone stranded at an airport—his tie was loose, he needed a shave. He was holding a turtle the size of a dinner platter in his lap.

The receptionist looked just as tired. His eyes were heavy and dark. He needed a shave too. He handed Dave a form and said, "It's seventy-five dollars for an examination. Treatment, if he needs shots or anything, is extra."

Dave paid the seventy-five dollars.

The receptionist said, "The vet is trying to save a budgie. It could be a while."

He stood up and looked over the counter at Arthur and he brightened for the first time.

"Hello there," he said softly.

Arthur, who hadn't taken his eyes off the moving cardboard box, twisted around. His tail began to wag.

The receptionist walked around the counter and kneeled down, scratching Arthur behind the ears.

"Yes," he said. "Yes. You're a good boy." Arthur rested his head on the receptionist's knees.

The receptionist smiled and looked up at Dave. "I had a dog just like this when I was a kid.

"You're a good puppy," he said turning back to Arthur. "It was just the greatest dog in the world. I was sick once and it wouldn't leave my room." Arthur was lying down now and the clerk had his hand buried in his belly. "My parents had to bring his food upstairs to my room. He wouldn't leave. You don't get that kind of loyalty from the people in your life. No matter how much they tell you they love you."

He stood up suddenly. "You fill out the form," he said. "I have to weigh him." He took Arthur away.

As Dave watched Arthur limp off, he felt an intense wave of affection for the dog. He turned and began to scratch his name onto the form. Suddenly the notion of banishing Arthur to the yard seemed cruel—as foolish as sending one of his children to sleep in the garage. No wonder Arthur's leg was bothering him. He wasn't young any more. The chill of the night ground would make anyone's legs ache.

The receptionist was back in under a minute. He handed Dave Arthur's collar. He was shaking his head.

"He had his front leg shoved right through this. I don't know how he managed that. It was so tight I had to cut it off. It's amazing he could even walk."

Dave took the collar and stared at it stupidly.

The vet walked into the front office and looked around.

"Who's next?"

Arthur was standing by Dave, holding his paw up, examining it as if he had never seen it before.

Dave looked down at his dog and then back at the vet.

But the vet wasn't looking at Dave, he was already bent over, patting Arthur. Looking down at the top of the vet's head Dave noticed a dramatic comb-over.

"What a prince," said the vet.

"I think they were before me," said Dave, looking at the two men in the waiting room. The man with the turtle had fallen asleep, the turtle was moving ponderously down his outstretched legs towards the floor.

"They're waiting on blood tests," said the vet, standing up. He walked over to the sleeping man, picked up the turtle and turned it around so it was crawling up instead of down the man's legs.

"Follow me," he said to Dave.

Arthur loped into the examination room beside the vet, his tail thumping.

"What's the problem?" asked the vet.

Dave said, "I just uh . . . I just wanted . . . uh . . . I just wanted you to check him over. He has been a little . . . listless."

He looked down at Arthur.

Arthur's tail was wagging furiously. He looked anything but listless.

The vet lifted him onto the examining table, looked into his eyes, his ears, his mouth. Listened to his heart.

"He seems fine now," he said. "Do you have air conditioning at home?"

"It hasn't been working properly. At night," said Dave.

"It could be the heat," said the vet. "Keep him out of the sun. Give him lots of water."

Dave nodded. "I'm sorry," he said.

The vet looked puzzled.

"Bringing him here. At this time of night. For nothing. I'm sorry."

"Don't be silly," said the vet. "There is nothing wrong with worrying about your pet. It's not owners like you who owe me an apology." The vet was washing his hands. "I just wish everyone cared enough about their animals to bring them in before real problems develop. You wouldn't believe the things I see some nights. You wouldn't believe how some dogs are treated."

Outside, Arthur looked up at Dave, his tail wagging. Before they pulled out of the parking lot he licked Dave's hand.

They passed a Dairy Queen on the way home, and Dave pulled over. Dave had a vanilla milkshake. Arthur had a soft cone with sprinkles and nuts.

When they got home, Arthur checked his bowl and finding it empty, headed upstairs.

He was lying in his basket when Dave came up. Dave looked at him and at the vent in his bedroom. He began to shut the bedroom door and then stopped.

Instead he went downstairs and fetched an electric fan from the basement. He set it on his bureau, turned it on and crawled into bed. Morley was already asleep.

"We're back," he whispered. "Everything is fine."

Twenty minutes later Arthur opened one eye. Lifted his head and looked around.

Galway

Galway, the cat, arrived in Dave and Morley's life courtesy of Dave's sister, Annie. Annie left Galway with Dave when she returned to Nova Scotia after living in and around Boston for almost a decade.

The cat, lean and beige, arrived with an ominous warning. "I don't like to say this out loud," cautioned Annie, "but whenever the cat's around, things seem to go wrong."

Annie named the cat Galway after the American poet Galway Kinnell—a gesture of affection for the poet's work.

It didn't take long, however, for Dave to recognize that the cat, either by coincidence or some quirk of destiny, had a poet's sensibility—being shy, to the point of misanthropy, and failing, in any real sense, to make connections in her new family. She terrorized Arthur, the dog, picked on Dave and largely ignored Morley and Stephanie. Only Sam, then nine, seemed able to meet Galway on equal ground.

One thing that leads a person to poetry is an inner life of some activity—often even turbulence. There is a weight of emotion, a burden of feeling that has to come out.

Galway had been living with Dave and Morley a year before she began to overgroom. Dave isn't sure when it began. One day, in the middle of the winter, he noticed Galway had licked the hair off both her front paws. It was not long after when he noticed there were bald spots on her hind legs.

The vet suggested the sleepers.

"Those little one-piece pyjamas," he said. "The ones you put babies in. With the snaps. Cut out the legs. And a bit at the back. So . . . you know."

Dave said, "You're kidding."

The vet said, "It will stop her licking."

Sam thought Galway looked cute in the pyjamas. "She looks like a monkey," he said. "I've always wanted a monkey."

Galway thought otherwise and disappeared. She was somewhere in the house—she emptied her food dish during the night. You could sense her shadowy presence, but no one saw her.

"It makes you wonder," said Dave, "if there are other animals moving around the house you never see."

Galway reappeared abruptly after a week. One evening while Dave was watching television he looked up, and there was Galway smouldering hatred from the top of the bookshelves. She was still wearing the jammies, though the legs were frayed at the bottom and chewed through at the knees. She had been rubbing at the only fur available—the fur on her ears and the back of her head. She had gone completely bald. In the ripped and threadbare pyjamas and with her rat-like head she had the threatening menace of a skinhead.

She was still around the next morning, but she didn't acknowledge anyone. And she began grooming again. She started with the little balls on Stephanie's chenille bedspread. In two days Galway licked Stephanie's bedspread flat. One night Morley got up, went to the bathroom and caught Galway grooming her toothbrush. It took Morley two seconds to teach the cat not to do that again.

She moved on to Arthur. One afternoon Dave came home and found the dog splayed out on the floor with Galway perched on his back, grooming his ear. Arthur, who habitually rushed to greet anyone who walked through the door, looked at Dave self-consciously, then sighed contentedly and dropped his head back to the floor.

"I don't think she's necessarily *crazy*," said Dave. "Maybe not even neurotic. I think she's bored. I think she needs a challenge."

And that is when Dave decided to toilet train the cat.

"If I'm going to take the time to teach her things, they might as well be useful things. Anyway, it's a skill that seems to dovetail with her interests."

Dave had seen something on television about a cat who could use a toilet. He figured it wouldn't be difficult to train her. Like teaching any animal a new trick, the most important part would be to move slowly. The most important part would be patience.

He decided the first step would be to move

Galway's litter box out of the basement. He would do it in stages, so he wouldn't upset her.

He set the box in a corner by the back door. Galway spotted it at dinnertime. She stared at it for a full minute. Then she walked slowly across the kitchen, down the stairs and dumped on the floor where the litter box used to be. She stared deliberately up at Dave while she did it.

"I was moving too fast," said Dave. "I tried to take her too far too fast."

He took the litter box back downstairs, but not to its original position. He set it a couple of feet closer to the stairs.

It took him two months to coax the box, and Galway, out of the basement, through the kitchen, up the stairs and into the upstairs bathroom. By April, Galway was doing her business in the cardboard litter box in the bathroom right outside Dave and Morley's bedroom.

The next step was to lift the box from the floor to the top of the toilet. If he could get Galway to use the box while it was perched on the toilet, Dave figured it would be nothing to cut a hole in the bottom and eventually get rid of it altogether.

"No more kitty litter," he said one night ebulliently. "This is actually going to work out."

He believed that.

Not wanting to repeat his earlier mistake, Dave decided to move the box up to the level of the toilet seat by imperceptible degrees. Once he got it to the right level he could slide it over and onto the toilet. He chose May 1 as the day for the beginning of the ascent. On May 1 he balanced the litter box on a couple of books and waited to see what would happen.

What happened was Galway looked at her litter box and then dumped in the bathtub.

"You have to expect setbacks," said Dave, the optimist.

"Not in my bathtub I don't," said Morley.

But Dave didn't give up. By mid-June Galway had stopped overgrooming. By the end of the month most of her hair had grown back and, to everyone's surprise, she was jumping, albeit resentfully, into her litter box, which by then Dave had perched on a stack of books, beside the toilet, at seat height.

"We're almost there," he said one night. "On July 1, I'm going to tie the box onto the seat. I didn't really believe we would get this far."

When July began, Dave had the box resting on the toilet seat with a hole cut in the middle and, to everyone's amazement, Galway was climbing into the box and doing her business through the hole. She was also scratching the wallpaper off the wall next to the toilet.

"It's instinct," Dave explained patiently one night to Morley. "She's wired to cover up her business as soon as she's through."

So Dave tried to be there for her—to be there to flush as soon as she was done. It seemed to be the least he could do. He tried to impress on everyone how important this was—to be there to flush when he couldn't.

Before long Galway stopped scratching the wall.

Then one evening they were downstairs eating supper and the upstairs toilet flushed. Everyone stopped and looked at each other.

Morley said, "Who was that?"

Dave said, "Sweet Jesus," dropped his cutlery and lurched upstairs. There was Galway, standing in her litter box with her head at the hole, watching the water swirling around in the toilet below her.

Who would have believed it?

Dave was ecstatic.

He was home free.

He would keep enlarging the hole and trimming the sides of the box until all that was left was a cardboard toilet seat cover. Eventually he could do away with that. Then maybe he would write a book. A bestseller. Get rich. Who would have guessed?

Then, out of the blue, disaster struck.

It struck at ten one night while Dave was watching the news on television. The toilet flushed and Dave looked around. Morley was beside him. Sam was in his room. Stephanie was out. The small smile that was tugging at the corner of Dave's mouth widened.

Pride before the fall.

As Dave sat in front of the television feeling prideful a hideous shriek filled the house. It was a piercing shriek of desperation unlike anything Dave had heard in his life—a howling, yowling, wailing wall of terror.

Morley reached over and gripped Dave's arm. The shriek was so horrifyingly loud that it lifted the hair off both their necks. Dave thought, *There's a maniac loose upstairs hacking someone apart with an axe*. Except it sounded worse than that, worse than murder. So desperately worse that it was no longer the sound of murder—it was murder itself. Murder was in his house and it sounded *just like someone trying to flush a cat down the toilet*.

Dave said, "Oh my God."

He pried Morley's hand free and flew up the stairs.

Sam was on his way down. His eyes bulging.

"THERE'S A HUGE SEWER RAT CLIMBING OUT OF THE TOILET," he shouted as he pushed past his father.

Dave threw himself through the bathroom door.

He had to look twice to be sure it *was* Galway. The bottom of the cardboard litter box had given way just as the toilet had flushed. Galway had fallen into the toilet at its fullest. She had plugged the hole so the water in the bowl couldn't escape. She was drenched, her wet, matted hair pressed to her rat-thin body. The toilet was slurping and sloshing and overflowing. Galway was yowling and clinging to the rim as the centrifugal force of the water slowly dragged her around the bowl.

Dave watched her make one complete rotation, and then—without thinking—he reached down to pull her out.

He had heard all the warnings about going near drowning people. He had missed the ones about

drowning cats. When he reached into the toilet,
Galway sank her claws into his wrists. Dave screamed
and flung the cat over his head, launching her the
length of the hall. She landed in a soggy and pathetic
pile of wet fur in front of Sam's bedroom door. She hit
the ground running. They didn't see her for another
week.

Sam was furious at his father.

"I don't know what was wrong with the pyjamas,"
he said. "I don't know why you had to throw her like
that."

Stephanie thought the whole thing was stupid.

Morley didn't say what she thought. Not directly.
She did ask pointedly about the wallpaper—more than
once. Each time she did, the conversation ended badly.

I told you so. That's what Dave heard. *I told you so*.
From all of them.

He threw in the towel. All he had to show for his
months of patience was a sullen family and a resentful
cat. He put the litter box back in the basement.

Galway began flushing the toilet again in the autumn.
She didn't *use* it, mind you. Wouldn't even get on the
seat. She would hop onto the bathtub and jump onto
the sink. From there she could reach over with her
front paw, push the lever on the toilet and stare at the
water as it went around and around.

"She always liked that part," said Dave.

Galway's fascination with the flushing toilet
seemed harmless enough—until Arthur started getting

into the act. Arthur and the cat would get in the bathroom together, Galway would flush and Arthur would bark his approval.

Then the toilet started overflowing. They had the plumber in twice with his Roto-Rooter, but it kept clogging up.

Stephanie blamed Sam.

"It's always after he uses it," she said.

Sam blamed Stephanie.

Dave suspected them both. Until one night he went to brush his teeth and caught Galway red-handed. He watched her swat a sponge off the window ledge and into the toilet. Then she flushed, her head circling around and around following the sponge. Dave managed to scoop it out of the water at the last moment.

It explained both the clogged toilet and all the little things they were missing: bobby pins, toothpaste tops, a bottle of Aspirin.

He cleared off the top of the tank. And the window ledge. He instructed everyone not to leave anything on the edge of the sink.

Then Arthur became her accomplice—bringing her things. One night after supper Dave caught Arthur mooching towards the bathroom with the TV remote hidden in his jowls.

The family began closing the bathroom door. For a few weeks Galway sat and stared at the closed door in indignation. Sometimes, in the middle of the night, she would sit in front of it and yowl. But they didn't give in.

Eventually she forgot about it.

So did everyone else.

Which is why no one thought to tell Dave's cousin Brenda that she should keep the upstairs bathroom door shut the one night she slept in the house alone.

Like Dave, Brenda was born in the village of Big Narrows, Cape Breton. She came to Toronto in September, for the first time ever. Against her will.

Brenda and her father, Ralph, drive the one and only cab in The Narrows. Ralph drives the morning shift, Brenda takes over in the late afternoon and will answer calls all night. In Big Narrows that means her last call can come anywhere between eight in the evening and dawn—which doesn't bother Brenda. When she doesn't have a fare she goes home and watches TV— or plays bridge on the Internet. Everyone knows where to find her if they need a cab.

Brenda is famous in The Narrows because she played centre on the town's Bantam hockey team when she was in grade eight—something that no girl had ever done before. It was the last time the team had made it to the provincial championships in Antigonish.

Brenda could do all sorts of things that other girls couldn't do. Of course the other girls didn't have the advantage of having their mother skip town with a member of the Norwegian merchant marine, as Happy McDougall did when her daughter was eight years old. Certainly the other girls didn't have the advantage of growing up under the baleful eyes of the three McDougall boys—Collum, Damon and Doug.

And so Brenda came to play hockey, and could put a worm on a hook with the ease most girls gave to tying shoes—reaching right into a can of worms with her whole hand. She knew about all sorts of boy things, like ball bearings and the difference between grease and oil.

When she was twelve Brenda discovered the Jumping Cliff behind the Macaulays' farm. The moss-covered cliff face was at least twenty-five feet high. It was Brenda who worked out that if you stood at the top of the cliff you could grab the branches of any one of the hundreds of maple saplings that grew along the cliff base. And it was Brenda who discovered that if you grabbed on to one of the saplings and stepped off the granite rock, your body weight would tip the sapling over and you could ride it to the ground.

Brenda learned this by accident on a Saturday afternoon she and Collum had gone trouting at the Macaulays' pond. On their way home Collum said he was going to cut off all her hair and she started to run through the woods to get away from him. When she came to the cliff face she did what Butch Cassidy and the Sundance Kid did when they were cornered on a cliff in much the same predicament—she launched herself into space. She grabbed one of the saplings on the way past. It was more of an afterthought than anything—her only real thought was keeping herself, and her hair, out of Collum's hands. She was amazed at how smoothly she rode the sapling to the base of the cliff. Collum, who watched her with equal amazement, tried to follow her down, unfortunately choosing a sapling that he thought looked like a safer bet—an older tree with a thicker trunk. Instead of bending gracefully under his weight and lowering him to the forest floor, Collum's tree waved back and forth like a metronome and then returned to the upright, leaving him treed like a frightened cat—too far from the cliff to jump back and clutching branches that were too small to climb down. When Brenda appreciated Collum's dilemma, she stopped running and walked back to the tree. She climbed onto a huge rock and listened to him bellow at her until she got bored. Then she went home and had lunch. She returned three hours later with a rope, only agreeing to chuck it to Collum and pull him back to the cliff after he had given his solemn promise to leave her hair alone.

Brenda waited two months before she showed the Jumping Cliff to anyone else. She spent hours there all alone—dropping gracefully from the cliff top to the forest floor. She learned by hard experience that if you chose a too-small tree you would crash to the ground as if you were riding an out-of-control elevator. And she learned that if you reached for a sapling that was growing too far from the base of the cliff and pulled it back and jumped, it would whiplash you like a catapult and you would fly through the air with alarming speed.

She found a beech sapling that was just far enough from the base, and one week she used it to launch every boy on her hockey team off the cliff—bringing them up there one by one and coaxing them onto the tree—*You aren't chicken are you?* Watching them shoot through the forest like screaming cannonballs.

She was furious at them because they had been too embarrassed to let her play in the provincial championships. She was their second-best centre, good enough for games on the island, good enough to help win them a berth in the provincials, but they were too embarrassed to travel to Antigonish with a girl on their team, so she had to stay home. They lost every game, which served them right, but she wasn't happy until she launched each and every one of them off that beech.

After she had got that out of her system, she used to go up there with gangs of boys every spring, when the trees were full of sap and flexible—Brenda and the boys climbing the cliff and flying through the forest like monkeys.

You couldn't help loving a girl like that. Well, not love. No one ever tried to kiss her or anything. They liked her too much. It would be like kissing your best friend. Like kissing your sister.

She was accepted at two universities—Mount Allison and Dalhousie. She chose Mount Allison because Halifax was too big. Her father drove her to Sackville in the taxi. She got a small apartment not far from Mel's Tea Room. She wrote to her father once a week and said she was happy. But she was home before Thanksgiving.

Her heart turned to stone on the morning of her first class—sitting in a cavernous lecture hall surrounded by a hundred people she didn't know. It gave her the creeps. Back home she had rarely been in a room where there was *one* person she didn't know. At least in The Narrows she knew who was decent and who was a jerk. It could take years to figure that out just for her English class. She went home and said university wasn't for her, and she started driving the cab at night.

She wouldn't have come to Toronto on her own accord. Brenda gets nervous whenever she has to go to *Halifax*. But she won a return ticket in the Elks' meat raffle—it was third prize. First prize was a quarter side of beef dressed and freezer wrapped, second prize was a bottomless coffee cup at June's Cafe. Just her luck to win *third prize*—a return flight to Toronto.

Whenever Brenda thought about going to Toronto, she started to sweat—all the traffic and people pushing around you. You could get swallowed up in a city like that and never be heard of again. Brenda imagined there were plenty of people from Cape Breton who had gone to Toronto for a visit and were now walking around aimlessly, looking for a way home. Too polite to ask directions.

One night she was lying in bed worrying, tossing and turning, and thinking of all the things that could go wrong, when the worst of all possible thoughts occurred to her. She phoned her father in a panic. "What if I like it?"

She wouldn't have gone if she could have got out of it. But everyone knew she had won the ticket. She landed at Pearson Airport at nine in the morning, exhausted from the effort it took to get the plane off the ground. She had no idea flying was so tiring.

She arrived so exhausted that the next morning, a Saturday, when Dave and Morley announced they had planned an overnight trip to Stratford, to the theatre, Brenda asked if they would mind if she stayed home, alone.

She wasn't crazy about the idea of being alone in the city, especially at night. But she wasn't crazy about getting back into a car either. The drive from the airport had been fearsome. Cars and trucks hurtling at them from every direction. There were eighteen lanes of traffic.

"I'll feed the cat," she said. "I'll walk the dog."

Arthur had taken to her instantly—following her around from room to room, settling at her feet. When she said the magic *walk* word, Arthur cocked his ears and sighed, his tail bouncing off the floor. Brenda reached down and ran her hand down the back of his neck.

"Good dog," she said. She found him comforting.

Galway, on the other hand, had given her a wide berth. Brenda had never been crazy about cats. The feeling seemed mutual.

She listened politely when Dave gave her directions to a neighbourhood cafe.

"It has a patio," said Dave. "It's a perfect place to sit and watch the city go by."

Yeah sure. Like she was going to go out at night alone.

As soon as everyone left, which was two in the afternoon, Brenda locked the doors and checked the windows. She made her supper—Kraft Dinner—and went to bed at nine o'clock, which was really ten o'clock her time.

It was unseasonably warm for late September. It all seemed surreal to Brenda—the leaves were gold and orange, the days short, yet the air in the bedroom was almost clammy. She got up to open the window, but as she stood in front of it with her hand on the latch she stopped and shook her head. Who knew what might happen if you did that? She went downstairs and made sure the stove was off. She got up a half-hour later to check the back door and then she lay in the stuffy bedroom with her eyes screwed shut and her fists clenched, following each police siren to see if it was heading her way, monitoring all the strange noises of this strange house.

She fell into a restless half-sleep shortly after eleven. Just after midnight she woke up with a start, her heart pounding, when—*the toilet flushed!*

Brenda had read how some burglars leave unspeakable things behind them before they flee the crime scene. She had never read about burglars who used the toilet before they began. Just her luck to get a weird one.

She lay in bed motionless—so rigid she was barely touching the mattress any more. Maybe he would go away. Maybe he didn't know she was there. If he came in her room she would start snoring. She would try to sound like a man.

The toilet flushed again.

Suddenly Brenda understood what was going on. Of course he knew she was there. That wasn't a burglar in the bathroom. It was a killer. He wasn't going to the toilet. He was sending her a message. He was going to kill and dismember her. Then he was going to flush her down the toilet.

Brenda did the only sensible thing she could think of doing under the circumstances. She jumped out of bed, clamped her eyes shut and leapt out the bedroom window.

Dave's neighbour Jim Scoffield, who happened to be sitting in his backyard, smoking a cigarette and enjoying the warm evening, looked up when the window exploded. He said it was the most remarkable thing he ever saw in his life.

"At first I thought it was Morley," he said. "I was sitting there and all of a sudden out she flew. I thought it was a gas explosion. I thought maybe I was next."

Brenda landed on the roof of the gardening shed in Dave's backyard. She landed on her feet, like a cat, and stood there, looking around. She had a few cuts on her arms, a big bruise on her shin, a sprained ankle, but nothing serious.

Jim looked at her across the fence. They made eye contact, and then they both looked up at the same time at the broken window she had sailed through. Galway was standing on the window ledge flicking her tail at the moon. Jim and Brenda looked at the cat and then back at each other.

Still they hadn't said a word.

It was Jim, who comes from the Annapolis Valley, who spoke first.

"Nice night," he said.

He came over and helped her down from the shed roof. She was wearing a pair of flannel pyjamas she sometimes wears when she takes the cab out in the middle of the night, so she didn't feel completely uncomfortable to be out in them.

They went inside together to look for the burglar but only got as far as the kitchen. That's when Brenda mentioned the toilet flushing. That's when Jim told her about the cat.

"Do you want a cigarette?" he asked.

She thought, *Do I ever,* and said, "Sure."

Jim went to his place to get his cigarettes and came back with a sweater for her, a beer for each of them and a plate of cheese and crackers. They sat in the backyard for almost three hours—found out that they had both dropped out of Mount Allison the same autumn. By the time they said good-night Brenda had decided she liked the way the Toronto sky didn't get night-black, didn't mind the river of faraway voices and car sounds that played constantly in the background.

When Dave and Morley got back on Sunday afternoon Brenda was sitting in the backyard, Arthur at her feet and Galway in her lap. She said she was extending her visit by a week.

To no one's surprise Jim announced in November that he was going home for Christmas for the first time in years.

"It'll be good to see everyone," he said. "I'm planning to get out to the island for New Year's. Maybe visit Brenda."

For her part Brenda told everyone in Big Narrows that Toronto wasn't so bad. That it's easy enough to meet people in Toronto.

As long as you go out at night.

The Fly

The small pleasure of going home at lunchtime is one of the welcome dividends that comes with owning a second-hand record store. When you choose to paddle in the backwaters, people don't get too bent out of shape when you pull to shore from time to time.

Dave closes his store and goes home for lunch a couple of days a week. It is the one time he can count on being home alone. Which—being the father of a teenage daughter—is a small pleasure he is thankful for. Most of all Dave enjoys getting to the mail before anyone else—sorting and reading it while he eats a sandwich or a bowl of soup.

Dave keeps a collection of smudged notes, hand-written on cardboard, taped to the inside of the front door of the Vinyl Cafe, which he uses whenever he closes during the day: "Back in fifteen minutes"; "I'm at Kenny Wong's" (that's Wong's Scottish Meat Pies, five stores along the street); "Gone to the bank." He has been using some of these notes for years—and a few of them are so smudged that Dave is the only one who can read them any more. He sticks them up, nevertheless, and customers who find the store locked when they thought it would be open peer at the black smears taped to the glass, and often try the door several times before they wander away.

Of all the notes, Dave's favourite is a sign he *didn't* make himself. It's a sign Morley gave him when he opened the Vinyl Cafe—a cut-out of a raccoon wearing a beret and smoking a cigarette. The raccoon has movable arms that you set like the hands of a clock. It's wearing a sweatshirt that says "Back At!" You position the raccoon's hands to tell when that will be. Dave uses the raccoon when he closes at lunch.

Dave came home for lunch one day in the middle of the week and found an envelope of the kind he is always hopeful of finding. The sort of letter that is the reason he bothers to check the mail. An ivory envelope of fine quality. Best of all, it was addressed to him.

As he carried the envelope into the kitchen Dave dropped the rest of the day's mail absentmindedly on the coffee table. A handwritten personal letter is not the sort of thing that you see every day of the week. It gave him pleasure just to hold it. So much pleasure that instead of opening it right away he set it aside while he made himself a sandwich—grilled cheese. Dave is old enough to know that the jackpot of anticipation is always a grander prize than truth affords.

As he cooked his sandwich he kept glancing at the ivory envelope. He didn't recognize the handwriting. There was no return address. He had no idea who might be writing him like this. Whoever it was had

used a fountain pen. It was a touch that implied inti-
macy, a kind of extravagance—something an old girlfriend might do. Dave carried his sandwich to the
table, ate half, wiped his hands carefully on a napkin,
picked up the letter and slit it open.

Dear Dave,

The salutation had been handwritten in the same ink
as the address on the envelope, but the body of the
letter was typed. Printed actually. It appeared to be a
form letter.

There is no disappointment as painful as the fall that
comes from great expectations.

Dear Dave,

   *This letter began five years ago in a small
village on the coast of Turkey. It was written by a
woman who lost her husband and children in a
horrible traffic accident. Since she wrote this letter
it has travelled around the world five times. It has
brought fortune and good luck to those who have
received it and have not broken the chain. A lady
in Brazil received a copy of this letter in 1997 and
she sent copies to relatives and friends. Within a
week she won a lottery and now lives in a large
house in Miami Beach. A dairy farmer in Britain
threw his copy out and England was eliminated
from the World Cup.*

   *You must make five copies of this letter and mail
it to five friends or neighbours within forty-eight
hours. You do not have to send them anything else.*

*If you follow these instructions good fortune
will occur within a week. However, if you throw
this letter out, or forget to forward it, there is no
telling what horrible thing could happen to you.
One elderly lady in Arizona made five copies and
put them in her purse, but she forgot to mail them.
Everyone who lived in her retirement community
began to speak in a strange language that no one
else could understand. Do not tempt fate. Continue
the chain.*

The letter was unsigned. Dave examined the envelope again. The handwriting looked vaguely familiar,
but Dave couldn't place it. He got up from the table
and carried the envelope and letter across the kitchen
and dropped them in the garbage can. He washed the
dishes and went back to work.

But the thought of the letter tugged at him all afternoon. Dave knew perfectly well that making five
copies and sending them to his friends wasn't going to
bring him good luck. It was the bad luck he was
worried about. England *had,* after all, been eliminated
from the World Cup. Dave didn't want to wake up one
morning speaking a language no one understood.

That night he pulled the letter out of the kitchen
garbage and flattened it and folded it and stuck it in the
pocket of his pants.

It's a hard world. You can't be too careful. It's not
such a big deal to make five photocopies. And even at
forty-six cents, a stamp is still a bargain. Dave went to

bed feeling better—so good that he completely forgot about the letter until he found it, a week later, when he reached into his back pocket looking for his wallet.

Dear Dave, Do not tempt fate. Continue the chain.

The same frustratingly familiar handwriting. But Dave's forty-eight hours of grace were up. He *had* broken the chain—there would be no letters from him.

The lingering urge to pass the letter on was a defensive urge—an evasive action. Dave knows he is never going to win the lottery and live in Miami Beach. He is comfortable with that, with the knowledge that he is *not* a winner. But he is also just as determined not to be a loser.

Dave was on his way to work when he found the letter in his pocket. And it was with some anxiety that he walked to the corner and dropped it into a garbage can by a telephone pole. As he did that, Dave sighed; it was a deep sigh of resignation, followed by a long deep breath. Which was, as far as he can remember, the moment he inhaled something.

Something that wasn't air. Something bigger than air. Something big enough to drive every thought out of his mind and send him reeling across the sidewalk, coughing. Tearing. Sputtering. Pedestrians were gaping at him as if he were having a heart attack. Surely not now, he thought. He was not even fifty. But for a moment, for a minute, for a couple of minutes—minutes he spent wheezing and coughing, minutes that he couldn't remember any more—for this eternity, until he could breathe again and was able to wave everyone off *(No, no. I'm all right),* for this lifetime, Dave thought he was about to die.

Something had gone down his throat. Something big. Something like a watermelon. Except watermelons are smooth. This was . . . rougher. More like a coconut. Except bigger than a coconut—this thing that nearly killed him.

When he was able to collect his thoughts, when he had collected himself, reassured the people who stopped to help him and wiped his eyes on the tail of his shirt, Dave tried to work out what had happened. The last thing he remembered, he had dropped the letter into the garbage can on the corner. He looked over at the metal container. At the garbage spilling over the top. At the flies buzzing around.

I just swallowed a fly, he thought.

His hand flew up to his chest involuntarily. He took a few tentative steps away from the garbage can. Everything seemed to be working all right—his legs were working. He coughed gently. He took a few more steps. He shrugged and began to sing softly to himself.

I know an old lady who swallowed a fly.

That made him feel better. He smiled, and started to walk a little faster. Still somewhat unsure, but the unsureness was now joined by the giddy relief that descends upon the survivors of major disasters.

He had almost died. He was alive.

I know an old lady who swallowed a fly.
I don't know why she swallowed the fly.

This event, this brush with death, had happened not far from the Vinyl Cafe, almost in front of Kenny Wong's restaurant. Dave thought maybe he should get a pop. Rinse his mouth.

As he went in, he debated whether he should tell Kenny what had happened—whether there was any shame attached to swallowing a fly. He decided it was something he *could* speak of. So he did. And when he stepped back on the street he felt a whole lot better. Walking to work. Singing.

I know an old lady who swallowed a fly.
I don't know why she swallowed the fly.
Perhaps she'll die.

And he stopped dead.

As he stood on the sidewalk halfway between Kenny Wong's restaurant and his record store the awful possibility hit him like a sledgehammer in the stomach. Maybe he didn't *swallow* the fly. Maybe he had *inhaled* it. Maybe the fly wasn't in his stomach—where it would drown and be eaten by stomach acid and disposed of in the most fitting of all possible fly burials. Maybe the fly was in his lungs—where there was oxygen. Where it could presumably . . . live. And lay eggs.

It was Dorothy at Woodsworth's Books who once suggested Dave should have changed his marriage vows from "in sickness and in health" to "in sickness and remission." She had a point. There is no denying that Dave has, over the years, waged more than his share of battles in the struggle for survival.

The war began when he was a child.

It began the summer afternoon he noticed his kneecap was loose. He was seven years old, attending a school swim meet, sitting in the stands in his bathing suit with his hands on his thighs when he stood up to see over Nancy Miller's head, and discovered that if he pushed down on his leg with his hands his kneecap moved back and forth under his skin. He looked around to see if anyone else had noticed. Then he went to the boys' locker room and locked himself in a cubicle so he could check out just *how* loose it was. It was alarmingly loose. He suspected that it was probably like a loose tooth and that he should leave it alone because the more you wiggled it, the looser it would get. He was worried that it might fall off. But once you discover something like this about yourself, it is hard to leave it alone.

Six months later when he went for his polio booster Dave showed his loose kneecap to Dr. Art Ormiston. Dr. Ormiston examined it carefully and acknowledged that there was no question it was moving around. Then he patiently explained that a kneecap wouldn't likely fall off. There was all that skin to hold it in place. Unfortunately he went on to tell Dave that from time to time people's kneecaps could dislocate. Dave looked puzzled. "Slip out of place," said Dr. Ormiston.

It took Dave no effort to imagine his kneecap slipping out of place. He imagined it sliding down his leg under his skin like a falling egg. In his imagination his kneecap ended up wedged in his ankle so he couldn't walk. He wore a Tensor bandage around his knee all that spring, only giving up when summer came and he had to wear shorts.

When he was eleven Dave got a sore in his mouth that hurt whenever he touched it with his tongue, which of course he did continually. Although he was ashamed of the sore, his curiosity soon outweighed his shame. He showed it to his father, who said it was a canker and that it would be over in a week at the most. Dave thought his father had said *cancer,* and understood that *he* was the one who would be over in a week. What he didn't understand was why his father seemed so offhand about it.

Later he learned about bacteria in health class. He began to hold his breath whenever he walked passed a sewer. He still doesn't inhale when he empties the garbage.

We all lug around baggage from our youth, and in the years that have accumulated since Dave was a boy he has become hyper-aware of the thousands of wily viruses and bacteria that orbit him like a family of organized criminals, sizing him up, preparing their move. He thinks of himself as a walking Petri dish, available for colonization by any one of the thousands of his microbic neighbours who may choose to move in. Knowing that at any moment he may inhale the wrong speck of dust and his face will begin to blow up like a balloon, or his capillaries will begin to leak blood and his crucial organs will pack it in one after another.

He takes as many precautions as he can without drawing needless attention to himself. He never takes painkillers when he has a headache, in case he might accidentally mask a massive stroke; and he knows the symptoms of most serious diseases, and many obscure ones. He knows how to disengage a hungry tick with a spot of whisky—which he long ago decided was a good enough reason to carry a flask wherever he went.

The notion of having a lungful of flies was not something he was going to shrug off. The notion of having a lungful of flies horrified him.

Perhaps she'll die.

Once again he was standing on the sidewalk, motionless, his hand on his chest.

What did the old lady do?

She swallowed a spider.

That wriggled and jiggled and tickled inside her.

She swallowed the spider to catch the fly.

There was no way Dave was going to swallow a spider.

It didn't work for the old lady anyway.

Perhaps she'll die.

Dave did not want to die.

Especially a trivial death.

"Unexpectedly, on his way to work, after a brief struggle with a chain letter."

A small part of Dave understood he was being crazy. Paranoid. He couldn't even say with certainty it was a fly he had swallowed, or inhaled. And there was a valve in your lungs that closed down when you breathed something in. Wasn't there? He was pretty sure it was impossible to inhale a fly. He might have swallowed a fly, but he was pretty sure he didn't inhale it.

He was also pretty sure he could feel it bumping against the side of his lung—as if it were trapped between two window panes.

He coughed as he unlocked the front door of his store. There was no one around. He left the Closed sign in place, locked the door behind him and stood despondently in front of the cash register. He looked around the empty aisles wondering what he should do. He could hardly go to the emergency department. He picked up a broom and began sweeping his way around the bins of records—pushing at the dust carelessly, trying to keep his mind off his lungs more than anything.

It didn't work. It was all he could think of. And pretty soon he knew with certainty the fly *was* in his lungs. He could feel it. It was a weird sort of buzzing sensation—a tickle that was less than a cough, but undoubtedly there. It wasn't normal.

By three o'clock Dave had worked himself into a complete lather. Maybe it was a fly that came into the country in a shipment of exotic fruit. A fly that carried an obscure disease that only a very few genetic types in all the world were susceptible to. And Dave was one of those people. They'd never diagnose that.

He would get a fever and go into a coma and then after a long and valiant fight in the hospital the fever would suddenly break and he would snap out of the coma but he would be speaking a foreign language that no one could understand. And everybody would think he had gone crazy.

Until an elderly Egyptian orderly recognized the language as ancient Sumarian.

It was six o'clock. Time to close the store. Dave wasn't sure if he should go home or straight to the hospital.

He went home. He took his temperature. Ninety-nine point two. Not a good sign.

Whenever Dave really starts to get into potential diseases, he likes to do Tai Chi. He only knows a couple of the movements but he repeats them over and over and they seem to centre him. Before dinner he went into the backyard and started to do Tai Chi. Morley has been around long enough to know what is going on when this happens. When she saw Dave in the backyard awkwardly spinning, stretching and bending she called out through the window.

"Dave," she said, "there's no such disease."

What did she know?

Dave knew he was going to die. The best he could hope for was that he might become a world-famous medical case and attract the attention of someone who could help him. Maybe along with the Sumarian he would develop the ability to solve complex mathematical equations, and Dr. Oliver Sacks would come from New York City to examine him. Dr. Sacks would watch Dave work out equations on a big blackboard in a university classroom and they would make a movie about him starring Robert Redford. Dave imagined himself going to the opening with his only friend in the world. The old Egyptian orderly. No. He would die before the movie was finished. He wouldn't get a cameo role, just a cryptic mention in the credits: *This movie is dedicated to the memory of Dave.*

He knew what he had to do and he knew he had to do it fast. He had to kill the fly. Until he killed the fly he was not going to be able to function as a normal human being.

The only thing he could think of doing was to cut off the fly's supply of oxygen.

Sadly, this was Dave's supply of oxygen too.

Working on this sort of medical problem—which essentially involves auto-surgery—is not something Dave likes to do at home in front of his family. He was too anxious to eat dinner.

"I'm not hungry," he said.

He told Morley he had to go back to work.

He let himself into the store and spent half an hour squatting on the floor behind the counter—trying to hold his breath for longer than a minute. Using one hand to squeeze his nostrils closed, and placing a strip of duct tape across his mouth, and kicking his feet as if he were being throttled, Dave was able to last a minute and fifteen seconds.

The problem was that after each attempt, he sucked in air so desperately and deeply that he was pretty sure that had the fly been trying to abandon ship it would have been driven back so far by the force of his inhalation that it would never find its way out again. He was pretty sure he could feel it reeling around his bronchial tubes like a drunk after an all-night binge.

That's when Dave realized the fly probably wanted out as badly as he wanted to get it out. They weren't enemies. They were partners. This is what people who run management seminars call "a shift in paradigms." Dave should help the fly, not punish it. He should show it the way home.

He stared at the table lamp on the counter beside the cash register. He removed the shade and flicked the light on. He slowly opened his mouth as wide as he could and began to sink down with his mouth wide open—trying to get his lips as close to the bulb as he could.

Which is what he was doing when his eyes caught movement at the front door. He looked up and saw Jim Scoffield staring at him, with *his* mouth hanging open, even wider than Dave's.

Dave straightened up and unlocked the front door.

"I was walking by," said Jim defensively. "I just happened to look in."

"I swallowed a fly," said Dave. "It's in my lungs. I thought it might be attracted to the light. I thought it might fly out to the light."

"That's moths," said Jim.

"What?" said Dave.

"Moths," said Jim. "It's moths that are attracted to light."

Dave stared at his friend.

"What are flies attracted to?" he asked.

There was a long and awkward moment of silence.

Jim said, "How do you know you have a fly?"

"I can feel it . . . it's a buzzing sort of feeling . . . like blowing on grass."

Jim said, "Do you have a vacuum cleaner?"

Dave glanced towards the back of his store.

Jim brightened. "We could use the crevice tool. The one for behind the radiator."

Dave said, "Are you out of your mind?"

Jim said, "You're the one with the fly in his lung."

Dave said, "I *do* have a fly in my lung."

Then he said, "Put your hand over my mouth and hold my nose so I can't breath." He started to turn around. "Don't let go unless I start to pass out."

Jim shrugged.

"Okay," he said doubtfully. He rolled up his sleeves and shifted his weight from foot to foot trying to find his balance.

He slipped his arms over Dave's shoulders.

"Wait a minute," he said, dropping his arms. "What do I *do* if you pass out?"

Dave turned around in exasperation. "You wipe your fingerprints off the door and go out the back so no one can see you."

Jim nodded earnestly.

Dave couldn't believe him. He was almost yelling now. "What do you think you do if I pass out? You give me mouth to mouth until I start breathing."

Jim cocked his head. "There's an idea."

Dave said, "What's an idea?"

"We could drown it," Jim said. "We could go to a pool and you could suck in a lungful of water."

Dave looked alarmed. "What about me?"

"We'll go to the Y," Jim replied calmly. "Where they have lifeguards. They'll know what to do about you. They're trained for that. You look after the fly—they'll look after you.

Instead of going to the Y, they went to Horgarth's Humidors. Dave bought a twelve-dollar cigar.

"I'll smoke it out," he said.

He chose a Cruz Real, number 19. Dark and sinister looking—like a burnt stick.

When he took it to the cash register, the man behind the counter tried to talk him out of it.

"That's a little on the strong side," he said.

"Good," said Dave.

"Actually," said the man, "it has a sort of numbing effect. You wouldn't want to smoke this cigar before a meal. It tends to remove your sense of taste for a couple of hours."

"Good," said Dave

"It is made in Mexico," said the man.

Dave smiled.

He figured there might be pesticide residues that would work in his favour.

"Anything else?" asked the man.

"A pack of matches," said Dave.

He lit the cigar on the street and took a long deep drag and held the smoke in his mouth. Then he inhaled it and nearly passed out. It was like the moment that afternoon, which seemed so long ago now, when he had inhaled the fly. He folded over as if someone had punched him in the stomach, and coughed for two minutes straight.

Jim stood beside him and said helpful things like "Are you all right?" and "I'm not so sure you are supposed to inhale those things."

When Dave stood up it was as if he was surfacing from underwater.

"I like these Mexican cigars," he said. "They have a sort of nutty flavour."

"Aren't you supposed to have a brandy with those things?" said Jim.

It was well after midnight when Dave got home.

He collapsed onto his bed beside Morley's sleeping form. He was still wearing his clothes and shoes. He did an inventory of his body. His head was throbbing, his stomach was somersaulting, but he couldn't feel any buzzing in his chest. To be perfectly honest he couldn't feel much of anything. Except bad. Except nausea.

When he closed his eyes, the room began to spin. He dropped a hand to the floor to steady himself. And that's exactly the position he was in when he woke up. At eleven o'clock the next morning—lying on his side with his mouth hanging open.

His lips were parched and cracked. His mouth felt as if it was full of ashes.

His head throbbed with pain.

Every few seconds a sharp noise bounced unpleasantly around his head. Whack. Whack. Whack.

It was like torture.

"Morley?" he said. Without moving, without rolling over.

"I phoned Brian," she said. "Brian opened the store."

Whack.

He rolled over.

Morley was poised by the window, a rolled newspaper raised in her right hand.

There was a fly on the window. Walking towards the ceiling.

Morley drew the paper back.

"I keep missing," said Morley.

"Wait," said Dave.

Dave inhaled deeply, and began to cough. There was a burning rawness in his chest, the feeling that his lungs had been seared by smoke—but no tickle, no buzzing.

"Don't kill it," said Dave. "Just open the window. It will go out by itself."

Morley shrugged and raised the screen. The fly circled the ceiling a few times and then darted out the window. Dave raised his head from the pillow and watched it disappear into the crisp morning air.

I'VE GOT YOU UNDER MY SKIN

Christmas Presents

One night at dinner, a Sunday night in late September, Morley pushed the dog's nose off the edge of the table, looked around and said, "I've been thinking about Christmas."

Dave gasped.

Well, he didn't really gasp. It was more a hiccup than a gasp. Although it *wasn't* a hiccup, and it could easily have been misconstrued as a gasp.

Everyone at the table turned and looked at him.

"Excuse me," he said. He smiled nervously at Morley. "I said excuse me."

Morley began again.

"I've been thinking about Christmas," she said.

"Me too," said Sam.

"And I was thinking," said Morley, "that it would be fun this year . . ." Dave was shaking his head slowly back and forth, unconsciously, staring at his wife while a confliction of emotions flickered across his face like playing cards—despair, hope, confusion and finally the last card . . . horror.

"I was thinking," said Morley, "it would be fun

this year, and more in keeping with the spirit of Christmas . . ."

Dave was leaning forward in his chair now, staring at Morley the same way Arthur the dog stares at the vet: with a doggish mixture of forlorn hope and wretched presumption.

"I was thinking," said Morley, "it would be fun . . . if we *made* presents for each other."

Morley's words met dead silence.

Then Stephanie dropped her fork.

"What?" she said.

Sam said, "Everything I want is made out of plastic. Does anyone know how to mould plastic?"

Morley said, "I don't mean *every* present. I don't mean we have to make everything. I thought we could put our names in a hat, and we could all draw a name, and we'd have to make a present for the person whose name we drew."

Sam said, "I like exploding stuff too. Exploding things are good . . . Especially if they are made of plastic."

Stephanie said, *"Gawd."*

Dave was nodding, a small smile playing at his mouth.

Two nights later Morley wrote everyone's name onto a piece of paper. She tore the paper up, folded the pieces and put them into a pot.

"No one say who they get," said Morley.

"What if you get yourself?" asked Sam.

But no one got themselves. And no one said who

they got. In fact no one seemed particularly *interested* in who got whom. Morley had hoped that everyone would be excited. But no one was, at all.

Several uneventful weeks went by, autumn settling gracefully on the city as the family settled into the routine of their lives. It was a beautiful autumn. An autumn for gardening and walks and stock-taking. The days were bright and blue, the leaves yellow (for weeks, it seemed). A forgiving, perpetual autumn. Until, that is, the winds began to blow. One night there was a storm, and it rained and blew, and the next morning the trees were bare. Soon the clocks were turned back, and a greyness descended on the city.

It was October and everyone was busy. Only Morley, who was the busiest of all, was thinking about Christmas. The night they had pulled the names out of the pot Morley had waited for the last piece of paper. When she unfolded it, she read her son's name. She had thought long and hard about what *she* could make a ten-year-old boy for Christmas that *he* would enjoy. And she was stymied. She didn't know plastics. She didn't know explosives.

Anyway she wanted to make her son something . . . meaningful.

Dave was no help.

"There's something about boys you have to understand," he said. "They *aren't* meaningful."

Nevertheless, Morley wanted to make Sam something he would treasure as he grew older. Like a fountain pen, or a fishing rod, or a National guitar.

She had wondered about a chess set for a while. She decided that although, with help, she might be able to make a rudimentary chess board, she would never, never in a million years be able to make the chess *figures,* and she had abandoned the idea of a chess set, along with sleeping bag, baseball glove and backpack.

The idea of building a chair for Sam came to Morley like a bolt out of the blue. She saw a brochure advertising a night course at the local high school. Ten Monday nights, two hundred dollars, all materials included. Morley checked the calendar. She would be finished a week before Christmas.

It was just what she was looking for—something she could make for Sam that he could use now, but something, if she did a good job, he could use for the rest of his life. Something that he might even hand down to his children.

Morley imagined building a big, comfy chair. A chair you could get lost in. She imagined Sam as a grown man reading the paper in the chair she had made. She imagined him surrounded by *his* family. She imagined him saying, "Your grandmother made this for me when I was ten."

She enrolled in the course and promptly missed two out of the first three classes. The first time it was work. The second time her mother had the flu. She had to take her supper.

She didn't miss any more after that. She applied herself as diligently as she could. And although every step was a struggle—each screw, nail and saw-cut a mystery of momentous proportions—and although her chair was emerging so much slower and tenuously than all the other chairs in the class, Monday, the night she got to work on it, became Morley's favourite night of the week.

She loved going to her chair class. The only thing that spoiled it was that no one else in her family seemed to have embraced the holiday project. She was alone on this Christmas journey.

She asked Stephanie about it one night.

"You don't understand," said Stephanie. "We're different, Mom. You're into the spirit of Christmas. I like the other stuff."

"The other stuff?" asked Morley.

"The shopping," said Stephanie, "the clothes."

"Shopping and clothes?" said Morley.

"And the TV specials," said Stephanie.

Then one morning, when Sam was getting up from the breakfast table, he looked at Morley and said, "I want to learn how to knit."

The biggest challenges of motherhood, for Morley, were always the surprises. She had long since abandoned the idea of priming herself for the next stage of her children's development. She had long ago accepted that no matter how she prepared herself she would always lag behind Sam and Stephanie. If Morley could count on her children for one thing, she could count on them to pop up, at the most unexpected moments, with the most bizarre ideas of life and how it worked. She could count on them to hold fierce opinions so contrary to what they had believed, even the day before, that they would leave her open-mouthed and totally unequipped to respond. Like the afternoon Sam had returned from the co-op nursery school and announced with quiet determination that he had "quit." Like when five-year-old Stephanie crawled, sobbing, under the kitchen table, and refused to come out until her mother promised never to serve hot dogs for lunch again. Never! *I don't believe you,* she sobbed, when Morley made the promise. Like the spring Sam developed a pathological fear of Big Bird, which became a fear of all birds, a fear that lasted for months.

And now he wanted to learn how to knit.

Morley had given up trying to teach Stephanie any sort of domestic skill. It had never occurred to her that Sam was the one who wanted instruction.

Morley gave Sam his first knitting lesson that night, in his room.

"Shut the door," he said.

She soon found out that teaching a ten-year-old boy to knit was about as easy as building a chair.

She didn't have the words for it.

She sat him beside her on the bed, and they both held a set of knitting needles out in front of them, as if they were about to fly a plane.

"Watch me," said Morley as she ever so slowly made a loop in the red yarn and slipped it onto the needle.

She was trying to teach him how to cast on.

She glanced at him. Sam staring at his hands in despair.

Morley took his needles and did the first row herself. She handed them back and said, "Okay. Now, do exactly what I do."

After an hour or so, he sort of had it. More or less.

"What is it you want to knit?" asked Morley.

"A coat," said Sam.

"Oh," said Morley.

Sam had drawn Stephanie's name.

Morley had to teach him again right from the beginning the next night. And once again two nights later. He did fine as long as he kept going, but every time he put the needles down he lost track.

By the beginning of November Sam was good enough to sit in front of the television and knit while he watched TV. Whenever Stephanie appeared, he would thrust the needles into Morley's hands or stuff them under the couch. Morley hauled an old black-and-white portable out of the basement and set it up on his bureau. He sat in his room all weekend, the needles clicking away like a train.

"My fingers hurt," he said on Sunday night.

The next Saturday he was invited to Jeremy's house for a sleep-over and he wanted to know what he could take his knitting in. Morley was afraid he would get teased, but she packed it up nevertheless, and he headed off with his toothbrush and his sleeping bag and his bag of wool. At nine o'clock Jeremy's mother phoned and said, "You aren't going to believe this. You know what they're doing? They're downstairs watching *Lethal Weapon Three* . . . and knitting."

Suddenly knitting was the thing to do. Suddenly *everyone* wanted to knit.

The next weekend there was a hockey tournament in Whitby. Dave drove Sam, Jeremy and two other boys.

"They all sat in the back," he said. "And they were talking about hockey and the game and how they were going to cream the team from Whitby—the kind of stuff you'd expect to hear from a backseat of little boys. And then one of them said, 'Damn. I dropped a stitch.'

"They'd talk about hockey some more. Then all you'd hear was the clicking of their needles, and then someone would say something like 'Look how long Jeff's is. Jeff, you're going so fast. You must have done this before.'

"It got quite giddy. One of them said they should knit on the bench between shifts. It was rather wonderful."

Morley didn't think it was wonderful at all.

As far as she could tell, her Christmas project was headed off the rails. She was *worried* about Sam. She thought he was getting compulsive about the knitting. He would disappear into his room and sit on the edge of his bed and knit for hours. And he kept unravelling everything he did. It was never perfect enough.

"It's fun to destroy it," he said. "I like the feeling of the knots coming undone."

It didn't seem healthy.

But that wasn't the worst of it.

On Saturday afternoon while Dave was in Whitby, Becky Laurence had shown up at the front door.

"Is Stephanie home?" she asked. She was holding a package wrapped in brown paper.

"No," said Morley. "Stephanie is out. Shopping."

Becky had turned to go, but then she had stopped and held the parcel up and said, "Tell her the present is ready. Tell her she owes me fifteen bucks."

She had shown up twice more that afternoon.

"Tell her I need the money," she said.

Morley was fairly certain that Stephanie had pulled Dave's name out of the pot on that night in October. And that placed Morley in a terrible position. She wanted to talk to Dave about what was going on. *Stephanie had paid her best friend to make a present!*— something so completely contrary to the spirit of the family that Morley had no idea what to do about it. But the present was supposed to be for Dave. And Morley didn't want to hurt him.

Anyway, as far as Morley could tell, *Dave* hadn't begun anything himself.

There was barely a week to go before Christmas, and her entire project was turning into a fiasco. *Her* chair was a mess. *Stephanie* was cheating. And Dave thought *Sam's* knitting compulsion was cute.

"Jacques Plante used to knit," he said.

"What?" said Morley.

"Jacques Plante was a goalie for the Montreal Canadiens," said Dave.

"I know who Jacques Plante was," said Morley.

"He was the oldest of eleven children," said Dave. "And they were poor. And his mother needed his help to make clothes for his brothers and sisters. When he was in the NHL he knitted his own underwear."

"What's your point?" said Morley.

"He said knitting calmed him down."

"You think Sam *needs* to knit?"

"I have a friend," said Dave, "who thinks the reason Jacques Plante was such a good goalie was because of all the knitting. He believes the knitting improved his hand-eye co-ordination."

That night, on her way to bed, Morley found Sam under the covers, knitting by flashlight. She went in and sat down.

"Are you all right?" she asked.

"My wrists are sore," he said.

The next night as she was preparing supper she could hear the knitting needles clicking against something.

When Sam came down for dinner he was wearing his skateboard wrist guards.

After dinner Sam called her into his bedroom. He was crying.

"I'll never finish the coat," he said.

He was pointing at the sum total of his knitting: a rectangle of blue wool about six inches wide and a foot and a half long. One side of the rectangle was completely asymmetrical. He didn't seem to be able to maintain constant tension as he worked. Each row was coming out a different length.

"It's . . . lovely" said Morley.

"No. It's not," said Sam. "I hate it."

He began to unravel it in front of her.

Morley brought Sam's chair home on the Monday before Christmas. The next night Dave found *her* in the basement crying. She had a bolt of beige corduroy at her feet. She was trying to tack a huge piece of foam to one of the arms.

Dave watched her for a moment without saying anything. Then he reached out and touched the top of the chair. The legs were uneven. It wobbled unsteadily.

"It's pathetic," said Morley, dropping her hammer on the floor.

"It looks . . . like it was made with a lot of love," said Dave.

"It looks like it was made by a two-year-old," said Morley.

"Well, it hasn't been covered yet," said Dave. "Any chair without upholstery is going to look . . . awkward."

"Pathetic," said Morley. "Not awkward." She picked up the hammer, swung it around her waist and laced the back of the chair.

"This is not working," she said. "Leave me alone."

Half an hour later she appeared upstairs, looking angry and defeated.

Dave looked at her. "I have a suggestion," he said. "Can I make a suggestion?"

Morley didn't say anything. But she didn't walk away.

Dave said, "You could spend the next few days down there wrestling with that material and you'll cover the chair, and we both know you'll end up with a bad chair."

Morley nodded.

Dave said, "Forget about the foam padding. Forget about the upholstery. Don't put fabric on it. Put wheels on it. What you have down there isn't a chair without covering. What you have down there is a go-cart without wheels. Put wheels on that thing and you will have one very happy little boy on Christmas morning.

And then he said, "I'm going to walk Arthur."

The next night after supper Sam called Morley into his room. He was frantic.

"The needles won't go through any more," he said.

He waved at a pile of wool lying on his bed—another six-inch square of knitting—each line of the square getting progressively tighter, giving the work the appearance of a triangle resting on its point.

"You have to relax," said Morley.

"I only have two days left," said Sam.

"Two days is not a lot of time," said Morley.

Sam nodded his head in vigorous agreement.

"But it should be enough time for a pro like you to knit a scarf," she said.

"I'm knitting a coat, not a scarf," said Sam.

"Oh," said Morley, "I thought you were knitting a scarf. Let me start it for you." Once again she began a row of stitches and once again handed it to her son. Then she stood up. "I have to do the dishes," she said.

On Christmas Eve, after Sam and Stephanie were in bed and the last present was wrapped and under the tree, Morley called Dave down to the basement. "Can you help me carry this upstairs?" she said.

She had taken the wheels off Sam's old wagon and attached them to the bottom of her chair. Dave climbed into it and smiled. She had left the wagon handle in place. It rested between his legs like a joystick.

"He'll love it," he said.

And then he screamed.

She was pushing him towards the washing machine.

First gently. Then faster and faster.

"Where's the brake?" is the last thing he howled, before he crashed into a wicker basket full of dirty clothes.

They could see light spilling out from under Sam's door when they went upstairs. They could hear the sound of his needles rocking together.

"He's still at it," said Morley. "What should we do?"

It was almost one.

"Come to bed," said Dave. "His door is shut. He wants to do this himself."

"He was working on a scarf," said Morley as she prepared the bed. "But this afternoon it changed into a headband. It wasn't going to be big enough to be a scarf. When I suggested headband, you know what the little bugger said? 'But isn't her head the fattest part of her?' It is the most pathetic headband you've ever seen. God, I hope she'll wear it . . . at least around the house."

"He's going to love his go-cart," said Dave.

Morley was sitting on the edge of the bed.

She turned around.

"Stephanie drew your name," she said. "There's something you should know about her present."

"No," said Dave. "Don't tell me anything. I want to be surprised."

Morley stood up and walked towards the bedroom window.

"Don't worry," said Dave. "It will be fine."

And so it was.

Stephanie, it turned out, had not paid Becky Laurence to make her father's present. She had written to her grandmother in Cape Breton and asked her to ship a photo of Dave and *his* father to the Laurences' house C.O.D. It was a photo that had amazed Stephanie the moment she saw it—which had been two summers ago—when she had gone to Big Narrows for a week by herself.

The picture was taken when Dave was five years old. In it, he is standing on the piano bench in the parlour, which makes him the same height as his father's bass fiddle, which they are both holding between them. And laughing—both of them—her grandfather's head moving backwards and to the side, her father (a little boy) starting to fold over at the waist, his hand moving towards his mouth. The way her brother's does in moments of hilarity.

The photo had haunted her for two years. The first time she saw it she thought the boy was her brother and the man standing beside the fiddle her dad.

"Where am *I*?" she had said.

She didn't believe her grandmother when she said, "No, no. The boy is your father."

When Becky Laurence gave her the picture, Stephanie took it to a photographer and had a copy made. She sent the original back to Cape Breton. She had her copy framed. It was wrapped and hidden in her cupboard two weeks before Christmas. Three times she had opened it so she could look at it. Three times she had to wrap it again.

But Morley didn't know any of this as she climbed into bed. As she fell asleep she was still worried about Christmas morning, about Stephanie and about the go-cart. She slept for a restless few hours, and then woke up. When she couldn't get back to sleep, she decided to make herself a cup of tea. She was almost out of the bedroom before she noticed the ribbon tied around her wrist. Red.

It ran to the floor, into a red pile, gathered at her feet. She was still dopey with sleep. She started to gather the ribbon up, and it was only as she did that that she realized it didn't end in the pile at her feet but continued towards the stairs. She followed it: down the stairs and past the tree and into the kitchen. By the time she got to the back door she had gathered an armful of ribbon. And she was smiling.

Dave and Morley have a pear tree in the corner of their backyard. Morley followed the trail of ribbon out the back door and across the yard to the pear tree. The end of the ribbon, the end not tied to her wrist, led to a switch fastened to the base of the tree. There was a note: *Merry Christmas. I chose you. Love, Dave.*

Morley flicked the switch. The most amazing thing happened.

The pear tree slowly and gracefully came to life.

Little lights began to snap on in the branches above her head and then, as if the tree had been animated by Walt Disney himself, the lights spread along the branches until the entire tree was glowing a dark red crimson, a crimson like dark wine, a red light that cast a magical glow over the backyard.

Dave woke at three and sensed he was alone in bed. He reached out his arm for his wife and didn't find her. He lay still. He tried to will himself awake. He got up and called her name. He walked to the back bedroom and looked out the window. Morley was sitting at the picnic table. She was wearing his work boots, the laces undone, and his winter coat over her nightie. On her head was a toque that belonged to Sam. She was cradling a mug of tea between her hands. From the perspective of the bedroom she looked twelve years old.

It had started to snow—big fat flakes of snow were dropping lazily out of the sky. Morley was staring at the snow as it floated out of the darkness and into the circle of red light.

Dave pushed the bedroom window open and said, "Merry Christmas." Morley bent down and made a snowball, glowing now as she stood in the red light of the tree, her hair wet and sticking to her forehead. She was working not so quickly that Dave didn't have time to gather a handful of snow off the window ledge himself.

The two of them threw their snowballs at almost the same moment, and they both laughed in wonder when they collided in mid-air, spraying snow like a shower of icy fireworks through the silence of the night.

Harrison Ford's Toes

If it comes at night, when you are sleeping, the first snowfall of the year can be an astonishing event. If you wake up on a September morning and walk to the window and throw open the blinds and find the world silent and white, you will, if you are lucky, be whisked back into a childhood world of wonder.

On a Thursday morning in late September, when she woke and saw snow on the ground, Morley stood by her window, taking it in, thinking eventually of her father and the skating rinks he used to make for her in their backyard when she was a girl. As she went downstairs to put on the coffee, she was wishing her father was still alive, wishing he could have met his grandchildren; wondering, as the aroma of the coffee filled the kitchen, if he were there, what she would make her father for breakfast.

Pancakes, said her father.

She was looking for the maple syrup when Dave appeared.

"Do you know where my blue sweater is?" he asked.

Morley had a dim springtime memory of folding sweaters and sealing them in cardboard boxes—but she had no memory of what she had done with the boxes.

This was dangerous territory.

If Morley said anything that implied the sweater might have passed through her hands while April passed to May, she would be opening herself to all sorts of liabilities. If she couldn't produce the sweater she was liable to be labelled a sweater thrower-outer, a sweater loser.

If, on the other hand, she was to deny all responsibility, she would be denying her image of herself as a wife and homemaker and mother. In her heart Morley *wanted* to be able to produce the blue sweater—she expected it of herself. That's what mothers do, she felt: they pull blue sweaters out of cardboard boxes the way fly fishermen pull trout out of mountain streams.

When it came to finding lost clothes, Morley was more a trawler than a trouter. She stood in the kitchen over her bowl of pancake batter imagining the impending search. She saw herself moving through the house like one of those draggers that scour the ocean floor looking for scallops—as likely as not leaving as much carnage behind her.

"Don't ask me about sweaters at breakfast," she snapped. "Unless they're made of maple syrup."

It was the only thing she could think of saying.

That night, after supper, Morley headed into the basement with a cup of coffee and a heavy heart. She chose the basement instead of the attic because it fitted her mood: it was dark, damp and as far from God as she could get without leaving the house. As she opened the basement door and stared into the gloom, Morley had a dim notion that this was the right direction—that down was the direction of redemption.

She put her coffee on the washing machine and stared at the pile of boxes along the basement wall.

That one, she thought, shrugging. The box was sealed with masking tape. As she pulled the tape loose it caught in her fingers. She rolled it into a ball. The ball stuck to her pants. She shook the ball loose. It stuck to her slipper. She stepped on it with the other foot, and it stuck there.

"Damn," she said, trying to kick it free.

She bent down and opened the carton—baby clothes. How had that box got to the top of the pile? It was not a good sign. It meant the boxes were out of sequence.

The next one was full of magazines. The one after that was a box of pants she hadn't worn in years. She was about to close the pant box when something in it caught her eye. There was something pushed down the side of the box—a package, about the size of an apple. She pulled it out. It was wrapped in green and red paper. There was a little card taped on one side. *Merry Christmas, Sam. Love, Grandma.*

Morley must have hidden it at Christmas. She had no memory of what it might be.

She sat down on a pile of boxes and reached for her coffee. She took a sip and opened the present.

It was a palm-sized plastic disc with a video screen—a miniature electronic game. It was the Tamagotchi Dave's mother, Margaret, had sent from Cape Breton.

Morley remembered now. Remembered the frustrating hours she had spent on Christmas Day searching for the Tamagotchi when it hadn't turned up under the tree. She hadn't wanted to give it to Sam. But she hadn't deliberately misplaced it either.

Funny, she thought, what the mind does. And totally in keeping with the way things were going that she would stumble on it now—now that Sam had clearly outgrown his interest. He was moving so fast. Even six months ago the Tamagotchi would have brought a whoop of delight. But her son had been going through a stage of toy divestiture. Across the basement there was a red plastic milk crate that Morley had carried downstairs herself not a month ago—Sam's collection of plastic dinosaurs. His Hot Wheels—his HOT WHEELS!—were in a similar box outside his bedroom door, waiting for the same sad, one-way trip. Music was his growing passion—the toy cars and the games of make-believe had been replaced by a Walkman—a depressing development that marked, as clearly as a mouthful of missing teeth, another stage of boyhood. It was a lurch towards adolescence that made Morley feel even worse about the Tamagotchi in her hand. Her little boy, her baby boy, was growing up—maybe if he had got the Tam he wouldn't have been in such a damn hurry.

Margaret had sent the Tamagotchi early that December.

Was it last Christmas? Or was it the Christmas before?

"I had to lie to get it," Margaret said proudly on the telephone.

"It's the last Tamagotchi in Cape Breton," she said.

Tamagotchis were a big deal that Christmas. Such a deal that they were hard to come by. Margaret phoned all over Cape Breton looking for one, and when she found a store with one left, she asked the clerk to put it aside, to hold it for her. They didn't do that, he said. In a moment of inspired improvisation Margaret appealed to the clerk's goodwill. She told him that her grandson was very sick, critically sick. The clerk put the Tamagotchi under the counter. You have to come today, he said.

When Margaret told her all this, Morley didn't know what to say.

Morley doesn't feel comfortable with those kinds of lies.

When it finally arrived in Margaret's Christmas package in early December, Morley worried that the Tamagotchi was jinxed. It would be tempting fate, she thought, to give Sam something that had been bought under those circumstances.

She agonized about this for days. How much easier she thought, if she had been born Catholic instead of Presbyterian. If she had been born Catholic she could have gone to confession—preferably in a church where they didn't know her—and she could have asked the priest where on the scale of mortal sins lying to store clerks ranked.

But Morley wasn't Catholic, so she couldn't talk to a priest. All she could do was talk to herself. And worrying that this awful little computer chip might be a death sentence, Morley had hidden it in the box of pants and, without intending to, had forgotten where she had put it.

She sat on her pile of boxes in the basement and stared at the toy. Then she did something that she was sure the priest would have told her was wrong. She ripped the plastic bubble off its cardboard backing and let the game fall into her hand. The screen was blank. There were two buttons underneath it. She pressed one—nothing happened; she pressed the other. Still nothing happened. She picked up the cardboard packaging that she had dropped onto the floor. There were no instructions written on it. Not even in Japanese. She looked at the toy again and pressed both buttons at once and two things happened simultaneously. A little egg bounced abruptly onto the Tamagotchi screen, and Dave appeared.

When Morley saw her husband walking across the basement, she slipped the Tamagotchi into her pocket. Maybe if she had already found the blue sweater she would have shared this discovery with him, but she hadn't, and he didn't need to know about it. He didn't need to know that *she* was the one who had lost the present his mother had sent Sam last Christmas—not now anyway. If she could lose track of a toy, she could, by extension, lose track of a sweater. She slipped the Tamagotchi into her pocket and looked around for cover—for something that might explain why she was sitting on a cardboard box in the basement.

The only thing within reach was the box of magazines. She picked a magazine out of the box, which happened to be *People* magazine, and which happened to have a picture of the actor Harrison Ford on the cover.

It was a casual photograph. Harrison Ford sitting on a porch—maybe at his home. He was wearing jeans and a black T-shirt and nothing on his feet. His feet were the closest thing to the camera. Morley was staring at the picture of Harrison Ford when Dave sat down beside her.

"He really is something," she said.

Dave sat down and peered at the picture over her shoulder.

"Even the scar is perfect," said Morley.

Dave squinted.

"On his chin," she said. "He had a car accident when he was twenty-one. He hit the steering wheel with his chin." She handed him the magazine. "Look at his toes."

Dave looked earnestly.

"They're perfect," said Morley. "He must have pedicures."

She wasn't thinking straight. If she hadn't been anxious about the sweater and preoccupied with the Tamagotchi, she wouldn't have said any of that. She knew that just as there are things that men can say among themselves in locker rooms, things that are all right to say when the only thing they are wearing is a jock strap and the only people listening are other men, so too are there things that can be said among women that should not, in the interest of long and happy marriages, be said at home.

She threw the magazine back in the box.

"Come on," she said. "Let's go upstairs."

It took an hour.

They were watching the news when Dave, without taking his eyes off the television, said, "What's wrong with *my* toes?"

Morley sighed.

"That's not what I meant," she said. "I said, I think he has pedicures."

"You said they were perfect toes."

"They *are* perfect toes," said Morley. "That's the point . . . I don't know men who have pedicures."

"If you are not attracted to Harrison Ford's toes, then why are we talking about them?" asked Dave.

"You brought them up," said Morley.

"No," said Dave, "I brought *my* toes up. You brought up Harrison Ford's toes."

"Because," said Morley. She was being very careful here. She was not going to have a fight about Harrison Ford's toes.

"Because," said Morley, "I've never heard of a man who has pedicures."

Then she said, "I think I would leave you if you started having pedicures."

Dave frowned.

"Well," said Morley, "I'd be awfully suspicious."

While she was getting undressed for bed, Morley remembered the Tamagotchi in her pocket and slipped it into her purse. She would dispose of it the next day—at work.

She crawled into bed beside her husband. The lights were already off. They were beside each other, but not together. Both of them lying on their backs, both of them staring at the ceiling, both of them absorbed in thought. Just as Morley was slipping away, Dave propped himself up on an elbow.

"Remember," he said. "Remember when I killed the snake last summer?"

Morley grunted softly and turned towards her husband.

"At the cottage," he said. "When I killed that snake?"

Morley nodded.

Dave said, "Harrison Ford is afraid of snakes, you know."

Morley raised her head. "What?"

Dave said, "It's like a phobia. He would be *chewing* on his toes if there was a snake in that picture on the cover of *People*."

Morley dropped her head down on her pillow. "Dave," she said, "that's Indiana Jones who's afraid of snakes."

The next morning, the morning after he had found Morley in the basement, Dave set off for work as usual. When he got there he began his usual ritual. He flipped on the lamp by the cash register, hung his windbreaker on the back of the chair behind the counter, dug the float out of a drawer—seventy-five dollars—and stuck it in the till, and he opened his coffee.

Dave is not really a coffee hound. There was a time, when he was on the road and still smoking, when he used to drink a lot of coffee. First thing he would do when he got up, first thing he did when he got to an arena, was have a coffee—*first things first,* he used to say.

These days he often doesn't drink coffee first thing in the morning, although he always has a cup when he gets to work. Sometimes he brews a pot himself. If he is walking, which he mostly does, he often picks up a cup from a diner along the way. He favours restaurant coffee—old-fashioned restaurant coffee served in thick porcelain diner cups, cups designed to hold the heat. There is something about the flavour of restaurant coffee, something about the colour and the taste. The coffee all the ubiquitous and trendy franchises push is too oily, too bitter, too expensive and, mostly, too complicated. Dave drinks his coffee black. If he is feeling like a treat, he might add cream—cream, not milk. He likes the way cream tastes. He likes the way it spiders into the coffee like ink in water.

Dave believes his morning coffee slows him down as much as picks him up. For Dave, the act of drinking is as important as the drink itself. It's a mental thing. It's about taking time, like stopping for breath. It's about *first things first.*

Sometimes Dave reads the newspaper while he drinks his coffee. Sometimes he just sits and thinks. Often he sits and doesn't think. This particular morning, he pulled a magazine out of his briefcase.

People magazine.

He had sneaked it from the basement on his way to work. He flipped to the cover story about Harrison Ford and scanned the pictures. He just about fell off his chair when he saw the shot from *The Conversation*—the chilling 1974 Francis Ford Coppola classic starring Gene Hackman was one of Dave's favourite films. He was only aware of Harrison Ford as Indiana Jones and Hans Solo. He was in *The Conversation*?

"What?" he said out loud.

How could he not know this?

He closed the article and studied the magazine cover. There was no denying Harrison Ford was a good-looking man. He flipped the magazine open and settled down to read the piece.

"No way," he said out loud a paragraph later.

No way Harrison Ford was nearly sixty years old.

No way a man ten years *older* than Dave could look that . . . good. And he did look good. He looked natural too. He didn't have that aura of artificial preservation that lingers around the likes of Dick Clark or George Hamilton.

"Jesus," said Dave a paragraph later.

He still smoked?

There had to be a mistake. He couldn't be sixty. It wasn't . . . *natural*. There had to be an explanation.

There had to be . . . liposuction? Steroids? Cosmetic surgery?

Three times that day Dave hauled the magazine out from under the counter and showed it to customers.

"How old do you think he is?" he asked Brian, stabbing the picture of Ford with his finger.

"Harrison Ford?" said Brian. "Got to love the man. Forty-five?"

"Exactly," said Dave. "Exactly."

That's what everyone thought.

"Guess what colour his eyes are?" he asked Brian.

"Blue?" said Brian.

"Hazel," said Dave. "And they change colour depending on what he's wearing."

"Jesus," said Brian. "Who writes *his* copy?"

About the same time Dave was flipping through the magazine with Brian, Morley was about to pay for her lunch at a downtown cafeteria. She was fumbling through her purse, looking for her wallet, when her hand landed on the Tamagotchi instead. How many times, she wondered, was she going to forget this thing? She pulled it out and stared at it. The egg she had produced by pushing the two buttons in the basement was rocking back and forth on the little screen. As she watched, it started to rock faster and faster. Then, right before her eyes, right in the cafeteria line—it hatched. Suddenly instead of the egg, there was a little creature pacing back and forth across the screen.

Morley was mesmerized. She stood in front of the cash register staring at the thing—the egg had hatched into a little animated chicken. The man in the line behind her said, *Excuse me,* and pushed by her. Morley barely noticed. The little chicken looked out at her and chirped. And the most unexpected thing happened— Morley was hit by a wave of maternal instinct. She was forty-six years old. Her youngest child was ten. And she had just given birth again . . . in public. She looked around to see if anyone had noticed. She paid for her lunch and sat at a table in the corner.

Before she had a bite of her sandwich—chicken salad—Morley spent fifteen minutes playing with her baby. It took her five minutes of trial and error to figure out which buttons to press to feed it. A few more to figure out how to clean its cage. When she finally put the Tamagotchi down, she felt simultaneously proud and ashamed. She stuffed it back in her purse, ate her sandwich and went back to work. Twice in the afternoon she pulled it out.

Caring for it at work was easy enough. Caring for it at home was more complicated. She hadn't told anyone about it. How could she? As the days passed, the chicken got more and more demanding.

"Excuse me," she said two days later when it began to chirp while she was washing the dishes. She went to the bathroom and locked the door. She pulled the toy out of her pocket and pressed the buttons. She knew it was ridiculous, but she wasn't about to let a chicken starve to death in her house.

Twenty minutes later while she was straightening out the pile of shoes by the front door, the Tamagotchi chirped again. She was frowning as she headed back to the bathroom.

"Are you okay?" asked Dave, who was walking out as she was walking in.

Morley kept the Tamagotchi in her T-shirt drawer at night. It was night three when it chirped from the bureau. Dave, who was reading a magazine in bed, looked up, puzzled.

Morley said, "It's a stopwatch I brought from work."

She hopped over to the dresser, scooped her Tamagotchi and took it into the bathroom, carefully closing the door behind her. She looked at the chicken with exasperation.

"You can't be serious," she said. "I just fed you."

Dave was too busy with his own thoughts to wonder what Morley was up to. The picture of Harrison Ford on the cover of *People* had rattled him. He had brought the magazine home from work so he could study it. It was hidden under a pile of books on his side of the bed. The more Dave stared at the picture—the more he compared himself to Harrison Ford—the more he was forced to face the fact that he had let himself go soft.

Before he climbed into bed Dave had stood in front of the full-length bedroom mirror, wearing only his underwear. Turning sideways, he gazed at his belly in despair. Where had it come from? He didn't remember it sticking out like that. When he stared at his face in the bathroom mirror it seemed even softer. He put his fingers on his cheeks and pushed his skin up towards his ears. It made him look startlingly younger. He needed a facelift! He *was* getting old and soft.

Harrison Ford didn't look old and soft. Harrison Ford seemed to have defied the ravages of age. Harrison Ford seemed to have stopped time. To get even half as fit as Harrison Ford, Dave figured he would have to change his diet, hire a personal trainer and spend hours a day under a bank of sun lamps. Fat chance.

Far easier to wallow in a pool of self-loathing.

He was standing in the bathroom the next morning, brushing his teeth, staring down at his ugly feet and loathing them, when he realized there *was* something he could do. He pulled his belly in and hauled his shoulders back. If he couldn't have Harrison Ford's body, at least he could have his toes. He looked down at his feet again and wiggled them. Just as Betty Friedan had cleared the way for many women to walk proudly out of their kitchens and into the workplace, Harrison Ford had made it possible for Dave to have a pedicure. All he had to do was make sure it wasn't at some neighbourhood place where he might be recognized.

It was an impulse born as much from curiosity as insecurity. Dave knew Morley wasn't going to leave him because some movie star had prettier feet. It had just never occurred to Dave that a man could have his nails done. It seemed like a waste of money to pay someone to cut your nails—*If God had wanted me to have pedicures,* thought Dave, *why would he have given me teeth?*

When Dave got to work he hauled out the yellow pages. The woman at the first place said, "I don't know if we do men. No one has ever asked." There was no confusion at the second salon. "We do men's hands but not their feet," said the receptionist. And then she added mysteriously, "We don't wax men either."

It had taken Dave all morning to gather the courage to make these calls. But once he had started, nothing was going to stop him. He stared at the ads. "German pedicures," said the one at the top of the page.

"When do you want to come?" asked the woman. Dave did not ask what a German pedicure involved. He didn't want to look stupid.

He didn't ask about anything until it was way too late—until he was sitting in a chair so space-age and contoured that it might have been pried out of the shuttle. His feet were soaking in water, his eyes were glued to the woman who had introduced herself as Ulla. He watched Ulla's every move as she laid out an assortment of implements—tools that looked as if they belonged in a surgery. She plugged in what appeared to be a router, and plucked Dave's right foot out of the water.

"We begin," she said, "by grinding the calluses."

Morley had always said that having her feet done was "the best." Once when she said that, Dave had asked, "Better than a massage?" And Morley had said, "Way better. Better than anything."

Because he didn't tell Morley that he had gone for a pedicure, Dave was not able to ask her how allowing someone to work on the soles of her feet with power tools could possibly be thought of in the same context as a massage. The very idea that his wife could enjoy this cast her in a new and worrying light. *If this,* thought Dave, *what else?*

But he didn't tell her about the pedicure. Couldn't tell her. Not because his feet looked bad. Because they looked so darn good. They were the best-looking part of him. Dave didn't know that Ulla would put nail polish on his toes. His toes looked as though they had been Varathaned. They looked so much better than any other part of his body that they only intensified his shame.

And so he wore socks to bed. And when he wanted to check his feet—which he did frequently, because they looked so good—he'd go into the bathroom and lock the door and take his socks off. Once he took the *People* magazine with him and compared his feet to Harrison Ford's. He thought he didn't come out so bad. Maybe not Hollywood, but not Hamilton either.

All the time he was doing this—sneaking in and out of the bathroom with a nail file to do maintenance, or to have a quick peek—Morley was sneaking in and out of the same room to feed the Tamagotchi.

This went on for a week, both of them so self-absorbed they were totally unaware of the other's preoccupation.

Only Stephanie, who needed the bathroom more than either of them, seemed bothered.

"WHAT IS GOING ON?" she said one night, while Morley scooted in as Dave slipped out.

The first time Morley answered that question it was to a woman she had never met. It was a Friday night. She was grocery shopping. She was feeding the Tamagotchi as she moved down the cereal aisle, so she had her head down and wasn't paying attention when she knocked into the woman who was coming the other way. They smiled at each other and Morley ruefully held up the Tamagotchi and said, "My son's. Alien chicken."

"Let's see," said the women.

As Morley held the toy out, the chicken started to chirp.

"Don't worry," said the woman. "It requires less attention as it grows."

It was a true moment of motherhood.

It was the very next evening that Stephanie came downstairs wearing Dave's blue sweater.

Morley stared at her. "Where did you get that?" she demanded.

"It was in my drawer," said Stephanie defensively. "Why?"

That night as they lay in bed Morley reached out for Dave and said, "Do you remember last Christmas when I couldn't find the present your mother sent Sam?"

She got out of bed and opened her T-shirt drawer and picked out the Tamagotchi and handed it to Dave.

She showed him how she fed it and how she cleaned it and how she played with it.

As they sat there in their bed the toy started to beep.

"What else does it do?" asked Dave, handing it back.

"It beeps," said Morley, pushing the buttons expertly. "Then it dies."

She fiddled with the buttons for a few moments and carried it back to the bureau.

She came back to bed and snuggled up to Dave.

Ten minutes later the Tamagotchi began beeping again.

Morley started to get out of bed.

Dave grabbed her by the wrist and pulled her back.

"I have to," she said, trying to pull free. "I won't be able to sleep if I think that thing is going to die tonight."

"I'll get it," said Dave. "I always did the night feedings."

The polish on Dave's toes began to chip two weeks after his pedicure. The morning he noticed the first missing flake he thought of touching them up himself. He sneaked into Stephanie's room looking for clear polish. All he could find was blue glitter and black.

He considered buying his own bottle of polish, but decided against it. It didn't feel at all right. The polish, after all, hadn't been his fault—Ulla had applied it without asking. To go out and buy a bottle would make him entirely complicit. True, he had been enjoying the secret of his perfect toes—his feet had given him a ridiculous sense of sophistication and he wasn't in a hurry to let the feeling go—but he wasn't prepared to visit Ulla every two weeks and he wasn't about to start buying bottles of nail polish either. If this was how Harrison Ford spent his time, so be it. It was just a step too far from *The Temple of Doom* for Dave. Anyway, he couldn't wear socks to bed for the rest of his life— surely Morley would eventually notice. Dave didn't want to be there for that. What was the point?

He did go to the drugstore, however. He walked in one afternoon and quietly examined the bottles of polish. But he didn't buy any. Another day, on his way home from work, he passed a cigar store that had a little leather-cased manicure set in the window. He walked in and asked how much and the clerk told him, "Two hundred and fifty dollars, sir."

"Two hundred and fifty dollars!" said Dave.

"It's made in Germany, sir," said the clerk, who had made a move to fetch the case from the window but was now turning back to other things. More important things.

Dave wandered over and looked at the case again. It was such a perfect-looking thing. So perfect he was sure it would inoculate elegance through his entire being—if he owned this one thing, more than his nails would be better, his entire life would change. He, too, could be as elegant as Harrison Ford.

Dave desperately wanted to buy it. For a moment he tottered on the brink, thinking of the small but not insignificant pleasure it would give him to summon the smarmy little clerk and wave offhandedly at the window, as if he bought these sorts of things all the time. As if money was no object.

He bought a four-dollar cigar instead, and a little box of wooden matches, which made him feel swank enough, walking home in the evening sun, smoking his cigar—until it started to make him feel ill.

The very next morning, he dropped a milk case of records on his foot. The nail on his big toe turned black. There seemed no point in worrying about nail polish or imported manicure sets after that.

It was that same week that the Tamagotchi died. Morley was not sure why or exactly when. She was at work and something made her check, and it was gone. Just like that. No warning. She couldn't believe it. As she stared at the empty screen she felt like crying.

When she got home she began supper immediately. Once it was under control, she went into the backyard and dug a little hole in the corner of the garden where they had buried the guinea pig. She took the Tamagotchi out of her pocket. It was wrapped in a piece of Kleenex. She put it in the hole and covered it with dirt.

There was a time, and it wasn't so long ago, when mothers had to accept that they would have to do this for at least one of their children. Influenza. Scarlet fever. Tuberculosis. Morley put her hand on the earth and shook her head. *That* was why she felt like crying. She stood up and looked around the garden, at the light of the autumn sun playing on the last leaves of the pear tree.

"Jesus," she said.

She wasn't sure if it was a prayer or an oath.

She was remembering a tiny tombstone she had touched in a graveyard beside a stone church in a Newfoundland outport. She was thinking of all the mothers who had carried on. She was thinking of Sam and Stephanie.

"Jesus," she said again as she turned to go inside, folding her arms around her chest against the chill of the afternoon.

It was a prayer.

Dorothy

The phone started ringing in the middle of the night. Ten past four by the clock radio. Dave jerked up before the first ring ended, his eyes closed, his heart pounding, struggling for the bedside table, overshooting and knocking his reading lamp onto the floor. The lamp landed on the dog, who was curled up on the floor, dreaming of food. In Arthur's dream someone, a pair of legs—Arthur couldn't see the rest of the body—was opening a never-ending stack of cans and, out of each can, pulling a leg of beef of improbable size. The bones were being dropped, one after the other, onto the sofa in the living room—the sofa that Arthur was, under normal circumstances, not allowed to go near. When the lamp bounced off Arthur's rib cage he whooshed onto his feet, snarling, his head swivelling in all directions at once, determined to protect his mountain of bones from this thing that had dropped from the sky.

Dave shrank from the edge of the bed, out of Arthur's reach.

And the phone kept ringing.

Dave wondered, as he groped in the darkness, why this should be so difficult. To answer a telephone in the night. As he struggled closer to consciousness, it occurred to him that whoever was calling at this time was unlikely to be calling with good news.

A spasm of anxiety gripped him as his hand landed on the phone.

He lifted the receiver.

The room was suddenly and dramatically quiet. Arthur was heading for the stairs, glancing nervously over his shoulder, on his way to check the sofa. Morley was awake and sitting up, leaning on her elbow.

Dave chirped cheerfully into the phone. He tried to sound as if everything was okay. As if all he had been doing at four in the morning was sitting around waiting for someone to call.

"Hi?" he chirped.

There was no one there.

Just the unmistakable hiss of a long-distance line.

"Hello?" said Dave, quieter, his heart sinking.

Something horrible, he thought, had happened in Cape Breton. Someone was calling from Cape Breton with horrible news. His mother?

"Dave?" said Morley, reaching out her hand.

And then there was a voice on the phone, a voice with a British accent. "Hello? Hello. Is anyone there? HELLO. I'm coming to town in three weeks. HELLO. I was hoping I could stay with you. HELL-OH."

"Hello?" said Dave.

"I'm terribly sorry," said the voice, "but I can't hear a BLESSED word you're saying."

Dave said, "Who is this?" and the voice, which was a woman's voice, said, "I CAN'T HEAR A BLESSED WORD."

And the line went dead.

Dave hung up. He looked at Morley and he said, "I think cousin Dorothy is coming to visit."

Cousin Dorothy, from the village of Hawkhurst, South Kent, England. Dorothy who shouts instead of speaks. Overweight and overbearing Dorothy.

Dorothy is the warden of South Kent. She has a desk on the second floor of the Hawkhurst Post Office, where she fields complaints from irate hikers about farmers who have let their crops overgrow the public footpaths. When a complaint lands on Dorothy's desk she marches off to the offending field, and Lord pity the farmer who gets in her way.

"I sue farmers," she says. "I'm a right bitch."

Which is not completely true. Dorothy has *never* sued a farmer. She has never had to. The other wardens write letters to *their* farmers, and if the letters are ignored, initiate legal proceedings.

Dorothy has never needed to turn to the law, because Dorothy's farmers are afraid of her.

Early in Dorothy's tenure as warden, a farmer pastured his bull in an effort to discourage hikers from crossing his fields. Dorothy showed up after a few days, struggled over the stile in her wellies, marched up to the bull and clubbed it between the eyes with a cricket bat. The bull sank to its knees. Dorothy stood in the field, whacking it whenever it tried to get up. She stayed there until the stunned farmer appeared.

He looked at Dorothy and his cowering bull and said, "Wot's this then?" And Dorothy told him he had twenty minutes to get his bull back in the barn or she'd be clubbing *him*. Word of that sort of thing tends to get around a farming community.

Dorothy has never married and lives in a flat beside the butcher's. She is a fierce person, for whom the winds of passion eternally blow. A fervent monarchist, she began collecting royal china when she was a teenager. She specialized in Margaret. She amassed a mammoth collection of Margaret teacups, ashtrays and biscuit tins that became known in certain circles. Until Margaret divorced Lord Snowdon, and an indignant Dorothy sold her collection at auction.

She continued to defend the royals, however. When Mountbatten, her cat, died, she rushed out and bought two corgis. She named them Elizabeth and Philip. Then when the Camilla tapes were leaked, she washed herself clean of the lot of them. It was over in a weekend. She lugged her china to the dump, had her corgis put to sleep and began talking about Diana as if she were a potted plant. *If her IQ was ten points lower,* she was fond of saying, *they'd have to water her*. To her credit she didn't change her tune after the accident.

She filled the royal void by campaigning against the European Union and playing the soccer pools. She read all the football columnists in the *Daily Mirror* and subscribed to a number of dubious tip sheets.

She lost interest in football when she began ringing the bells at the village church. There were three other bell ringers in Hawkhurst. They practised Wednesday nights and performed on alternating Sundays. In the evenings she wrote lengthy rebuttals to the vicar's sermons, which she left on the pulpit each week after practice.

Dorothy was not technically Dave's cousin, but she was the only relative he knew in Britain, and it seemed important to maintain the contact. He visited her in the early seventies when he was travelling with a disastrous James Brown European tour. She turned down his invitation to the show, sniffing when he offered. He took the train down from London, and they met for tea and sausage rolls. She made it abundantly clear that the idea of "America," as she kept referring to Canada, held no interest for her whatsoever.

But Dave kept in touch, phoning whenever he was in England, and when he and Morley were to be married they sent her an invitation.

She didn't reply, but three months after they were married, a package arrived from Kent, a royal teacup, smashed into three pieces. It crossed Dave's mind that the cup might have been broken before it was mailed.

"I can't imagine," said Dave the morning after her call, "why she'd be coming."

She arrived three weeks later, on the 4th of August, on a charter flight that landed at four-thirty in the morning.

Dave was at the airport to pick her up.

Cousin Dorothy, now in her seventies. Tweed jacket, ivory blouse, wool skirt, sensible shoes. Wearing a pair of Mountie earrings. She was coming to Canada to attend a convention, a worldwide get-together for fans of the Canadian television show *Due South*.

They were meeting for four days at a downtown hotel.

"I didn't know they got that show in Britain," said Morley.

The first thing Dorothy said to Dave, as she stormed past the airport security guards, was not *Hello* or *It was good of you to meet me at the airport, in the middle of the night*—the first words she uttered when they met on the arrivals level at five-ten on that Tuesday morning in August were "After lunch we're going to meet the deaf wolf."

In *Due South*, the Mountie hero, Constable Benton Fraser, has a deaf, junk-food-eating pet wolf—played by a husky.

Dorothy was still talking about the wolf ten minutes later, after they had talked their way past the security guards and back into the luggage area to fetch her suitcase.

"His name is DIEFENBAKER," said Dorothy.

They were standing beside the carousel, waiting for her suitcase. GREEN, she had said.

"That one?" asked Dave, pointing hopefully at a small green suitcase rounding the corner.

Dorothy shook her head. No.

"DIEFENBAKER is his TELEVISION name," said
Dorothy. "The crew calls him O.T."

"What?" said Dave.

"O.T.," said Dorothy. "That's what the crew calls
the wolf. The dog, actually."

"What about that one?" said Dave, pointing at the
next green bag.

Dorothy shook her head again.

"O.T. is short for Overtime," said Dorothy.

Then she interrupted herself. "THERE," she barked.
"THAT ONE!" She was pointing at a huge *red* suitcase
coming towards them. It was hanging half off the
conveyor.

"THAT ONE," she said again, bouncing up and down.

"I thought you said green," said Dave.

"I know my own suitcase," said Dorothy, punching
Dave's shoulder as the bag rolled by them. "GET IT."

Dave grabbed the bag and jerked it off the belt. It
landed at his feet with a thud.

"Careful," said Dorothy.

When he tried to pick it up, he swayed unsteadily.

"Which way?" said Dorothy over her shoulder. She
was already walking. Barrelling off in the wrong
direction, heading back towards her plane.

Dave got her turned around and they set off for the
car, Dorothy two steps ahead and going maniacally
on about the dog, Dave struggling along, his left arm
extended from his body like a tightwire artist's,
counterbalancing the heavy bag that was bouncing
off his right calf with each step.

"The production crew gave him the nickname," said Dorothy.

They were halfway up a flight of stairs that seemed to stretch forever. Dave was paying more attention to the alarming acceleration of his heart than he was to Dorothy. He could feel the blood surging through his ears. He was wondering if he should stop and rest.

"O.T.," said Dorothy, "is short for Overtime. The husky they used for the first two seasons was so dumb it bungled every stunt. So they were always doing extra takes. Which meant lots of overtime for them. Let me take that."

She plucked the bag from Dave and swung it effortlessly up the rest of the staircase.

"Where's the car?" she asked at the top.

Registration for the four-day Friends of Due South convention didn't begin until that afternoon. It was only seven when Dave and Dorothy arrived home.

Morley said, "I'll fix tea."

Dave said, "I'll show you your room."

Stephanie was sleeping with Sam for the duration of Dorothy's ten-day visit.

"WE ARE GOING TO MEET THE DEAF WOLF AT LUNCH," said Dorothy to Stephanie as she dropped onto her bed.

"Oh," said Stephanie, who had given up her bedroom under protest.

Fifteen minutes later everyone was sitting around the breakfast table.

"I WANT TO GO SHOPPING FIRST," said Dorothy, who, unlike Dave, didn't seem any worse the wear from the night's flight.

When Morley set the mug of tea in front of Dorothy, bag in, Dorothy pointed at it in horror.

"What's that little bag?" she said. "What's THAT?"

"It's a tea bag," said Morley.

"No, no, no, no, no, no, no," said Dorothy. "Tea doesn't come in bags. Tea comes in a tea caddy."

"A tea caddy," said Morley. "What's a tea caddy?"

"A thing you put TEA leaves in," said Dorothy, leaning back in her chair and crossing her arms.

Dave went to the corner store to buy loose tea. Morley went to the basement in search of an old Brown Betty.

"And a tea cozy," said Dorothy after Morley. "We'll need a tea cozy."

"And a cup and saucer," she added, more to herself than to anyone else.

Then she looked up and smiled at Sam and Stephanie.

"I want to get one of those hats that Canadian snowboarder wore at the Olympics," she said.

"He was disqualified," said Sam. "For drugs."

"For *marijuana*," corrected Dorothy, reaching for a piece of dry toast. "Marijuana would *not* have helped his performance *one bit*."

Stephanie smiled at her aunt for the first time. "I'll take you shopping," she said.

When they were on the subway, Stephanie asked, "What is a tea caddy anyway?"

"It's a metal tin with a hinged lid," said Dorothy. "And a little silver spoon that says Best Wishes from Skegness."

An hour later Dorothy and Stephanie were standing in front of a mirror in a downtown clothing store. They each had a Canadian Olympic team hat pulled tightly down on their head. There was a bulge of red skin, like a rim, protruding from under Dorothy's hat and running across her forehead.

"What do you think?" she asked.

"Great," said Stephanie.

Dorothy was scowling. She was alternatively fiddling with the angle of the hat and the angle of the mirror.

"I never look good in hats," she said, shaking her head. She pushed Stephanie playfully on the shoulder. "But that snowboarder sure was drop-dead gorgeous."

That night Dorothy came home from the convention with a *Due South* poster and a Polaroid snapshot. She passed the photo around at dinner.

In the picture she had her arms around a large husky.

Dave glanced at the picture and handed it to Stephanie. When he looked back at Dorothy he noticed dog hairs on her blouse.

"A nice dog," she said. "I was thinking I could get one like him back home."

When they were finished eating, Morley brewed tea. She made a fuss of warming the pot before she added the boiling water. Then she self-consciously counted each teaspoon of tea leaves aloud so Dorothy could see she was doing everything properly.

". . . three, four and one for the pot."

After the tea had steeped for four uncomfortable minutes, Morley picked up the pot with a flourish and began to pour the steaming mahogany liquid into the china cup she had borrowed from Gerta Lowbeer.

Dorothy waited until she finished.

"My dear," she said. "We ALWAYS put the MILK in first."

Then she looked across the table at Stephanie. "If you don't put the MILK in FIRST, you could CRACK the cup."

Dave tried to show her around town.

He suggested a museum of Canadian art. He tried a historical tour. She wasn't the least interested.

"Do you know where they shot the headquarters?" she asked. "Do you know where his apartment is?"

Every night she had things to show them at dinner, more photos, souvenirs she had bought. And stories of her fellow conventioneers.

"I met a girl from the Philippines," she said.

Dorothy had spooned a mound of mashed potatoes onto her plate and was using her fork to work a wedge of butter the size of a cookie into the middle of the pile. Sam watched in awe as she turned her potatoes into something that looked more like pudding than vegetable.

"Her mother is dying of cancer," she said.

She was eating and talking. Loading her fork with potatoes and meat, waving it in the air while she talked and then popping it in her mouth during pauses when she might otherwise have breathed.

"It's funny," she said. "I have watched some of the programs fifteen times. I have them on tape. You get to know the dialogue.

"There is a show when Benny, he's the Mountie, when Benny is shot in the leg. At the end his friend Ray is teasing him. And Benny says, *'That's not amusing, Ray.'*

"After she told me about her mother, I looked at the girl from the Philippines, and I said, 'That's not amusing, Ray.' We both started to laugh and then we started to cry. It was very odd but it was very nice too. I felt like I had known her for ever so long."

That was the last day of the convention.

The next night at supper Dorothy seemed lost. She had nothing to tell them. As they were eating dessert, she suddenly said, "I had to sell jewellery to come here."

They all stopped eating.

"I sold a diamond ring and two gold bracelets," she said. "They were my grandmother's."

No one said anything. But she didn't look at all embarrassed.

"I'm not much for jewellery," she said. "I kept it in a box at the top of my cupboard. I never wore any of it. I hadn't even looked at it for years. So when I heard about the convention I thought, *I am going to turn those things into money*."

Stephanie nodded approvingly.

She had a week left before she had to go home.

Dave asked what she wanted to do.

"Niagara Falls?" he asked.

She shook her head. No.

An hour later she came downstairs and said, "I want to see a REAL Mountie."

Dave assumed a real Mountie meant a Mountie in red. The only place Dave could think of finding a Mountie in red was on Parliament Hill.

They left late on Saturday afternoon—Stephanie stunning her parents by announcing her willingness to come with them. It was the first family trip she had *offered* to be part of for over a year.

They left so late that Dave gave up on the idea of getting to Ottawa before dark.

They checked into a set of cabins on Lower Rideau Lake.

"If we get an early start," said Dave, "we can still have a full day."

The cabins were built in the thirties—white clapboard with a small screened porch, built in a semi-circle under a stand of pines.

Dave bought three beers from the woman in the office. They ordered pizza from the only pizzeria in the phone book. There was an above-ground swimming pool under the trees. Dave dragged three wooden

Adirondack chairs over to the pool and they sat there, Morley, Dorothy and Dave, and drank their beers while the kids swam.

They ate their pizza outside. A rusty pickup truck with a dumpy camper on the back bounced up to the cabin beside Dorothy's. The driver jockeyed the truck around the pines—he was pulling a boat in a trailer, a large indoor cruiser. When he parked, he climbed out of his cab and stretched.

He was wearing a plaid work shirt and blue jeans so dusty they were turning brown. He hadn't shaved for a few days. His cheeks were sunburnt, weathered. He smiled pleasantly and said, *"Bonjour,"* as he walked by them on his way to the motel office.

The sky was blue and grey and purple and orange— the light soft and dimming. The green neon No Vacancy sign flipped on. Dave looked at the sign and at the cars buzzing by on the highway. He felt relaxed and peaceful.

If it wasn't for the mosquitoes, it would have been perfect. The mosquitoes had come when they were eating the pizza.

"This is Canada," said Dave to Dorothy as he slapped at his neck. "Now you know what we're all about."

They went into Dave and Morley's room and watched a movie on television. Then they went to bed

"We'll start early," said Dave. Again.

Dorothy had a cabin to herself. She lay on her bed and stared at the water stains on the unpainted wooden ceiling. One of them reminded her of the Queen Mother. She began to organize the boards on the ceiling into groups of five, using her fingers to keep track. Then into groups of three. It was hard to concentrate. There was a rip in the screen in her bedroom window and her cabin was full of mosquitoes. She had never heard anything like it—the drilling buzz of the bugs as they dove around her head. She had to stop counting every few seconds and brush at her face.

At midnight she got out of bed and put on the red Mountie long johns she had bought at the convention. She stuck her head under her pillow, but the mosquitoes wouldn't leave her alone.

She didn't look at what time it was when she finally got up and opened the cabin door. The night was dark and starry. The pine trees stretched towards the stars like black towers. The air seemed thin and young. Dawn was still hours away.

The city had seemed like home, like a home away from home—but this was different.

She slapped at the bugs and, in an effort to escape them, began to walk around, trailing her hand against the things she passed—the picnic table, the Adirondack chairs, the wall of her cabin, the boat on the trailer in front of the cabin next to hers.

She walked around the boat three times. Moving faster and faster to stay ahead of the bugs. Marching almost. Singing. "Waltzing Matilda," of all things. She had to keep moving or the bugs were going to drive her crazy.

It was on her third trip around the boat that she noticed the ladder hanging over the stern.

She stared at it for a moment and without stopping to think climbed the four rungs and struggled over the transom onto the deck.

There was a door and three steps leading down into a cabin. It didn't feel as if she was doing anything wrong; it didn't feel as if she was trespassing when she opened the door and ducked down the steps. When the door closed behind her there were no bugs for the first time in hours.

She breathed a heavy sigh of relief and sat down on the bench. The next thing she knew she was dreaming of the ocean. Dreaming of the gently rocking sea. She was happy and sailing home on a rolling sea.

Eventually, however, the sea seemed to be getting rougher. As if maybe there was a storm, and she thought she should do something about that. Shouldn't she batten down the hatches or something? Wasn't that what you did when you struck stormy weather at sea? The boat was hit by a monstrous wave. A wave that washed over the ship and almost scuppered her.

She woke up confused—without the faintest idea of where she was. She crawled off the bench looking for a clue and then out of the cabin and onto the deck, standing there dazed in her red long johns, squinting in the bright morning light as the boat bumped by the motel sign.

She was just in time to see Sam, still in his pyjamas, standing barefoot on the dewy grass in front of his parents' cabin, rubbing his eyes, staring at her. She raised her arm, involuntarily reaching out for the boy, as if he might be able to rescue her. But as the trailer bounced over the gravel shoulder and onto the highway, she lost her balance momentarily and had to reach for the railing. When she looked up, she saw Sam holding his arm up too. Waving goodbye.

Dave got the licence plate number of the pickup from the motel register—Pierre Boisclair. He had marked his address Saint-Michel-des-Saints.

They waited at the cabins—Dave getting increasingly agitated with each passing hour. At noon he looked at the motel manager and, for the hundredth time, said, "Why hasn't she phoned?"

The manager shrugged. "I told you. I don't know. How could I know? Maybe they know. Maybe you should phone *them*." He was pointing to a pile of brochures for a psychic hotline.

Dorothy hadn't phoned because she was still trapped on the boat, which at that moment was swinging from side to side off the back of the truck as it rolled past miles of pine trees. The forest growing darker and thicker and closer to the highway with each passing minute.

Before long Dorothy found a cellphone in the galley kitchen and used it, but when she did, she didn't phone the motel where Dave was pacing, because she didn't have the faintest idea what the motel was called, or for that matter, where it was. Until she found the phone, however, all she could think of doing was huddling in the galley.

Occasionally one of the wheels of the trailer wandered off the pavement and bit sickeningly into the gravel on the edge of the road, and it felt as if the entire enterprise had had it, and Dorothy had to grab on to whatever was at hand or be thrown to the ground. The first few times this happened she cried out loud, but after a while she became used to it. She endured an hour of this and finally thought, *Enough is enough.* She decided to head onto the deck to see if she could attract the driver's attention.

Before venturing above, she strapped herself into two orange lifejackets, which she hoped would protect her if she was thrown overboard. She brought the first one down over her head, fastening it the way it was designed to be fastened, and stepped into the second and tied it around her waist like a diaper. Crawling towards the bow in her red underwear and orange lifejackets, she looked like some kind of a fungus moving along the deck.

She gave up before she got halfway and retreated below, this time finding the phone and a bottle of cognac.

An hour later she was back on deck—sitting at the tiller in her lifejackets—waving the bottle of cognac gaily at any cars that passed them on the highway. She was still sitting there when Pierre Boisclair pulled over on a deserted stretch of highway to have a leak.

"Bonjour," she said when their eyes met.

About the same time, Dave gathered everyone up and said they were going home.

"She's probably dead anyway," said Sam. "They probably had an accident and she's probably dead."

Everyone was pretty glum as they pulled out of the motel for the long drive home. Each time they passed someone pulling a boat, Stephanie strained to look inside, even though Dorothy had headed north and they were driving south.

"Maybe," said Sam, "he was some kind of weirdo. Maybe he's holding her somewhere. Like in a cabin in the woods or something."

There were three messages on the answering machine when they got home.

The reception on the first was terrible.

"For GOD's sake," it said, "I am in a BOAT on the HIGHWAY. And I don't have any clothes. HELP ME. Where are—"

And then the line went dead.

"There must have been a cellphone on the boat," said Morley.

The second message was clearer. "This isn't amusing, Ray," she said, and hung up.

The third had come just before they arrived home.

"All's well that ends well. I'll be back in a few days."

Dave slapped his head.

Stephanie smiled. "Cool," she said.

And then nothing.

Not another call.

Not another word.

Nothing.

For three days.

Dave got Pierre Boisclair's number in Saint-Michel-des-Saints from information, but when he dialled it there was no answer. He considered phoning the police but what would he tell them? Dorothy had sounded cheerful enough in her last message.

"Leave her alone," said Stephanie. "She's an adult. I wish I could live like that. Do what you want to do whenever you want to do it."

Dorothy returned the night before she was scheduled to fly home. She was sunburnt and happy.

"What are you all STARING at?" she bellowed after she walked through the door.

She didn't say much about her three days away. No one was game to ask for details. She had been fishing—that much was clear.

"Fresh pickerel," she said, "in butter over an open fire is something hard to imagine."

After dinner she said she had to make a phone call and she went upstairs where they wouldn't overhear her. Dave caught a few words in French. He heard her say, "In your dreams, Pierre."

The last Dave saw of Dorothy was at the airport. She was at the customs table on the far side of the security desk. It was just a glimpse as the frosted security doors were sliding closed. She was standing at a table talking to a cop, *RCMP*, thought Dave. Her suitcase was open and the policeman was holding up a red serge Mountie jacket that she had bought at the convention.

The way the Mountie was holding the red jacket between them brought to mind a matador at a bullfight.

"I wouldn't," he said quietly to himself, "wave that too quickly."

WHO'S SORRY NOW?

The Last Kind Word Blues

You can count on weekday afternoons to be peaceful at the Vinyl Cafe. Those languid hours after lunch until, say, four o'clock when the high-school kids begin drifting in are a reliably low-key time at the world's smallest record store. Kenny Wong says being in Dave's store after lunch is like being in the hole at the centre of a doughnut, which suits Dave fine.

Dave waits for the quiet of the early afternoon to eat his lunch, a lunch that never varies. Three sandwiches on sliced brown bread: one cheese, one peanut butter and one honey. The same three sandwiches he has eaten every day for the twelve years he has owned the Vinyl Cafe—the sandwiches cut on the diagonal, then stacked carefully in the same sequence and wrapped in wax paper. Every day Dave places his stack of sandwiches on the counter and works his way down one side and then the other—cheese, peanut butter, honey; cheese, peanut butter, honey.

"Cheese slices!" said his friend Alison the first time she saw this—so long ago the lunch was novel enough to warrant attention. "Cheese slices," said Alison, "aren't cheese."

Dave, who had just picked up a cheese sandwich when she said this, thrust it in the air between them and said, "I actually prefer the cheese slices with the plastic wrap left on." Then he bit into it with relish.

Whatever comfort Dave takes from his lunch is no longer a conscious comfort. It is a ritual that has become a part of him: an involuntary impulse that comes as easily as breath. He makes the sandwiches before he goes to bed and stores them in the fridge. The first time he forgot his lunch bag, Dave locked his record store and walked home in a fog to retrieve it. He found himself standing in the kitchen twenty minutes later, looking around, confused, not sure what he was doing there.

After he finishes his lunch Dave often reads for a while. Most weekday afternoons allow him this quiet, this peace, but if you wanted to choose one day out of the whole year and count on finding him with his nose in a book, you could do worse than bet on a rainy Tuesday in April.

It was on such an afternoon that Dave was sitting behind the counter with half of a cheese sandwich beside him and Nick Hornby's *High Fidelity* propped open on the cash register. He had Blossom Dearie on the turntable, and a cup of tea at hand. If anyone had walked into the store at that precise moment and asked how business was, Dave would have looked up in surprise. He would have set his book upside down on the counter, surveyed the empty aisles and said, Business is fine, thank you. Although he would have been thinking, *It was better before you came in.*

Dave shares a trait with many people who run second-hand stores, which is not widely seen elsewhere in retail. It is a characteristic that sometimes surfaces in librarians. Dave resents his customers. It's not that he doesn't like them. He likes the people who come into his store. What irks him is when the people insist on buying stuff, insist on leaving his store with records that Dave views as part of a private collection—his. If people came into his store looking for conversation rather than records, Dave would be a lot happier.

And so it was on that rainy Tuesday afternoon when Dave was lost in the Nick Hornby book that he didn't hear the front door open, or see the young man in the trench coat step in. Didn't notice him, that is, until he was standing in front of the counter, awkwardly clearing his throat.

Dave lookcd up.

"Can I help you?" he asked.

Under his coat the young man was wearing a blue suit, a white shirt and a bright yellow tie. If Dave could have seen the young man's feet he would have seen brown leather brogues, carefully polished. Not the typical customer who comes into the Vinyl Cafe, especially on a rainy Tuesday afternoon. He looked more like a corporate lawyer than a record collector, which, in fact, he was. The kind of man who might drive a small red car and own CDs, not vinyl, which was, in fact, the truth.

"You don't recognize me, do you?" said the young man.

Dave closed his book reluctantly, stood up and shook his head. "No," he said. "I'm sorry, I don't."

The young man, who Dave thought looked maybe thirty-five years old, leaned on the counter.

"Geechie Wiley," he said. "'The Last Kind Word Blues.'"

Dave stared at the young face blankly. He squinted and cocked his head to the side. He said, "My God."

The young man grinned self-consciously and looked down at his feet. "I guess I've changed a bit since I saw you last."

Dave nodded.

"Kevin Burnett," said the young man holding out his hand.

"I remember," said Dave.

The two men stared at each other silently, both thinking about the last time Kevin had stood where he was standing. It was also on a spring afternoon, a spring five, maybe six, years ago, thought Dave.

"Seven," said the young man. "I had just graduated. Lisa and I were engaged. I was on my way to Kingston . . . to article."

It was no wonder Dave hadn't recognized Kevin. He was still a boy seven years ago. In those days his soft brown hair brushed his shoulders. He wore an earring in one ear and three silver rings on various fingers of both hands. He favoured plaid shirts, blue jeans and work boots.

During the five years he lived in Toronto getting his law degree, Kevin Burnett had worked at a variety of jobs and spent a healthy proportion of his disposable income on music. He lacked the imagination of Dave's favourite customers: young men who pursued whimsical record collections—a football player who specialized in girl groups from the 1960s, an accountancy student who obsessed on Hawaiian surf guitar, a sociology drop-out who worked in a bookstore and was trying to assemble the complete K-Tel library from 1972 to 1976 and his very favourite, a history major named Derek who would only buy compilation records by "not the original artist."

Kevin just bought music he liked: folk, pop, a lot of rock and roll. But his enthusiasm for the music overcame his ordinary taste. He became a regular at the store, if not a respected member of the inner circle.

Until, that is, the April afternoon seven years ago, when Kevin walked in the front door of the Vinyl Cafe, carrying his entire record collection in four cardboard boxes. He lugged the boxes in, one by one, and lined them up by the cash register.

"Lisa and I are moving in together," he said. "We're getting married next spring." He motioned at the boxes of records on the floor and said, "I want to sell them."

Dave remembered this clearly. Remembered Kevin waving at his record collection dismissively. Remembered him saying, "It's time to move on. Time to grow up."

It wasn't enough that Kevin expected Dave to buy back every record he had sold him over the past few years, he was standing there implying—wait a

minute, he wasn't implying anything—he had stated
it. He thought there was something juvenile, something inherently immature about collecting records.
As if he was the adult, and Dave was someone who
had never . . . well, in his words, got going, moved
on. As if you couldn't own vinyl records and at the
same time be . . . grown up.

"Lisa has a CD player," said Kevin. "Soon there are
going to be CDS in cars."

Dave smirked.

"I'm serious," said Kevin.

Dave was thinking, *What about me? Am I not
serious? Am I not an adult? Have I not moved on?*
Then he settled on the most dangerous thought of all:
Is this what they all think of me?

Kevin lifted the first of the cardboard boxes onto the
counter. Dave reached for his calculator and began to
flip through the records. He had done this so often that
he could price them as rapidly as he could flip, which
is what he was doing until he was halfway through the
third box, and his hand suddenly hesitated. He looked
up abruptly. Kevin was behind the counter pouring
himself a cup of coffee. He hadn't noticed the hesita-
tion, or the look on Dave's face.

It was the look of astonishment. Dave couldn't
believe his eyes. He was staring at a record he thought
he would never see. Ever. "The Last Kind Word
Blues" by Geechie Wiley. Dave had been looking for
this record for twenty-four years, ever since the night
he last heard it—the only time he had heard it—on a .

jukebox in a beery roadhouse in the smoky hours before an Alabama dawn. Dave was driving the bus for a long-forgotten rock group touring the American South. They had a night between gigs and Dave had spent it feeding nickels into the bar's scratched and foggy jukebox. It was the only time in his life he had seen one that played 78s. He played the Geechie Wiley tune over and over and over until the bartender, a large sweaty, tattooed man wearing an undershirt, walked over and wordlessly yanked the plug out of the wall. He stared at Dave as he did it, daring him to say something.

"The Last Kind Word Blues" by Geechie Wiley. Dave had talked to collectors about the record. Not much was known about it—or Ms. Wiley—just that she was probably from Mississippi and the song was probably recorded about 1930. Someone had said there were only five known copies of "The Last Kind Word Blues" in existence. If this was the sixth it would be worth, in this condition, hundreds, maybe thousands, of dollars.

Dave had long ago given up hope of ever finding Geechie Wiley's record. He was sure he was dreaming. He closed his eyes. But when he opened them, he was still in his store, and "The Last Kind Word Blues" was still there on the counter. It was better than anything he could imagine. Better than a cheese sandwich.

He said, "I didn't sell you this record."

But when he spoke it didn't sound like him speaking. It sounded like someone speaking from inside a tunnel.

"I know," said Kevin, putting his mug of coffee on the counter. "I don't know where that record came from."

There were record collectors who followed the catalogues and would pay a lot of money for "The Last Kind Word Blues" by Geechie Wiley. But Dave wasn't one of them. Dave had never paid more than ten dollars for an album. Never charged more than twenty-five. It was a point of principle. He despised the collectors who bought and sold records the same way speculators bought and sold stocks. They were the same obsessive types who had stolen the world of hockey cards away from little boys, perverting an innocent schoolyard commerce with their greedy little catalogues. Most of them didn't even like music.

Dave totalled up the value of the records in the boxes in front of him; then he hesitated. What should he add for the Geechie Wiley record? He punched in twelve dollars. It was two dollars more than he had ever paid for an album in his life. He was breaking the ten-dollar barrier for the first time ever—a limit he had promised himself he would never exceed. But he had to make an exception. The dignity of the record demanded it.

He looked at the total. Two hundred and seventy-eight dollars for the four boxes. He measured his words carefully. "You might," he said, "be able to get more for some of these records at a collectors' show."

"I don't have time for that stuff," said the boy. "I trust you."

Dave grimaced. "You're sure?" he said.

The boy nodded. If he had asked, *Which record?* If he had asked, *How much more?* Dave told himself he would have pointed out the Geechie Wiley. Would have told him the catalogue price. But the kid was in too much of a hurry to grow up.

It wasn't a lie, but it was an uncharacteristic deceit. Dave was too elated to dwell on it. He felt as if he had won the lottery. He was whistling as he walked home, the record in his briefcase. Clearly it belonged with him, with someone who hadn't outgrown it. He would wait until everyone had gone to bed before he played it. So he could savour it, without distraction.

Morley was cooking dinner. He began to tell her what had happened as soon as he got in the door. He began by telling her about the night in Alabama when he had first heard Geechie Wiley. It was a story she had heard before. She was distracted with her cooking and, Dave sensed, uninterested. He changed the subject before he had to tell her the details of his purchase.

He didn't play the record that night. He intended to. Before he went to bed he took it into the living room, but when he got to the turntable he decided he should wait until he was home alone, so he could crank up the volume and there would be no danger of anyone disturbing him, no one asking him to turn the music down. So, he told himself, it would be a perfect moment.

Instead of playing the record, he played *with it*. It was a beautiful thing: ten wide inches of hardened shellac. He leaned it up against his turntable and sat down and stared at it. He looked around the room, trying to forget the record was there, glanced back and pretended to be surprised to see it.

"My goodness," he said to himself, as if he were someone else, a guest, a friend, a newspaper reporter writing a profile on record collectors. "You have a Geechie Wiley?" Dave nodded coyly. "Yes," he said out loud.

Then he frowned. It would be ostentatious to leave the record out like that for the reporter to see. As if it was on display. He tapped his fingers. Where did it belong?

He jumped up. Halfway across the room, he turned around. "Did I ever play you my Geechie Wiley?" he asked the empty chair.

He was doing the same thing he might have done with a pair of leather gloves left unclaimed at the end of a party, or with a cake plate abandoned after a potluck dinner or a book that had been on loan for too long to return. He was trying to work the record into his stuff.

He dropped it on top of the pile of his favourite albums, and smiled. "Have you ever heard Geechie Wiley?" he said to the reporter who was sitting in the chair and had morphed into Joni Mitchell, looking at him with wonder.

"You have a Geechie Wiley?" said Joni Mitchell, who was lighting a long, dark cigarette. "You certainly have one of the most incredible record collections I have ever seen."

"Dave?" It was Morley calling from upstairs. "Are you talking to me?"

"Just a second," said Dave to Joni Mitchell. "It's my manager."

Dave files his records alphabetically. "This is where you are going to live," he said to the Geechie Wiley as he dropped to his knees. "This is the Who and this is . . . my goodness . . . this is Weird Al Yankovic. Al, this is Geechie Wiley." He slipped the record into place. He was gloating as he headed upstairs to bed, intoxicated by his own sophistication, wondering what Geechie Wiley was going to make of Weird Al.

Halfway up the stairs he stopped and looked back.

"See you later," he said to Joni Mitchell.

Kevin came back to the store two days later.

"That record you asked about," he said. "The blues record. By Geechie Wiley?"

Dave's mouth dropped. Kevin thought Dave was confused.

"The one you asked about," he said again. "'The Last Kind Word Blues.' It wasn't mine. It belonged to Lisa's father."

Dave reached for the counter. He felt as if he was going to faint. He stared dimly at the boy smiling at him.

Kevin was saying, "That's why I didn't remember buying it. I never bought it. Lisa's father bought it. He wants it back."

Dave's eyes narrowed. He felt a flood of rage surge unexpectedly through his body. He hadn't even played it yet. He wasn't going to give the record up.

He said, "I've already sold that record."

"They didn't appreciate it the way I could," he told Morley that night. "If the girl's father understood what it was, the girl wouldn't have been running around with it. They don't deserve it."

Morley didn't say anything.

"What are you looking at me like that for?" said Dave. "I didn't steal it. I paid for it. I bought it. A deal's a deal. It belongs to me."

He no longer felt comfortable keeping the record at home. He took it back to the record store. And not knowing where else to put it, he took it upstairs to a storage room where he keeps odds and ends: boxes of old paper, piles of equipment, stacks of memorabilia from his days as a rock-and-roll roadie. But it was the only record up there. And it didn't fit. It wasn't memorabilia. It was music. And he still hadn't played it.

One lunch hour, Dave locked the front door of the Vinyl Cafe and put the Be Back in an Hour sign into the window. He went upstairs and fetched the record. When he came back he sat behind the counter where he couldn't be seen from the street and dropped it on the turntable. The opening chords of the song filled his head for the first time in twenty-three years. When the song ended Dave lifted the tone arm and set it down at the beginning. And then again.

The rhythms of Geechie Wiley's voice uncorked the bottle of time. Dave was hit by the same wave of emotion that had washed over him on that night in Alabama so long ago. Only this time he recognized the wave. This time he was old enough to give it a name. It was the wave of loneliness.

Once again the record had messed him up.

There was someone knocking on the door. Dave looked at his watch. He had been playing the record for over forty minutes. He turned off the record player, walked to the front and unlocked the door. While the customer wandered around the store, Dave absent-mindedly picked up a pencil and wrote "twelve dollars" on a little sticker and pressed it lightly on the top corner of the Geechie Wiley cover. It was the amount he had paid. He put an exclamation mark after it. He opened a drawer under the counter and dropped the record out of sight. It stayed there for eight months.

On a Saturday eight months later, a young Ryerson University student who had been working in the Vinyl Cafe for a few months found the record when he was looking for a pen. His name was Ken, and he dressed as if he had stepped out of the old *Leave It to Beaver* television show. Ken is the only part-timer Dave has ever fired.

It was many things. It was the records he played on the store's sound system for one. He began with stereo sound-effects recordings. Next it was a spoken-word record called *Two No Trump: Teach Yourself Bridge*, featuring Charles Goren. Ken would lay a deck of cards on the counter and inch the volume up if the store got busy. When Dave told him he was restricted to music, a rule he had never had cause to invoke before, Ken nodded earnestly. His favourite group turned out to be the dwarfs from *Snow White*. He would crank up the Disney soundtrack and bustle around the store filing records, whistling while he worked.

The Saturday morning Dave caught himself doing the same, at home—whistling while he washed the dishes—he vowed Ken would go.

Two weeks later Ken sealed his fate. Dave left him alone for an afternoon and he reorganized the front of the store. He moved stock around and took down obscure signs that had hung over obscure boxes of records for years. He cleared a table and began to refile records alphabetically, by artist. Ken didn't get it. Didn't understand that the organic confusion that is at the heart of the Vinyl Cafe is the thing that makes it work. Ken didn't understand that people don't visit the Vinyl Cafe the way they visit Wal-Mart. Dropping by the Vinyl Cafe is a hobby more akin to metal detecting than shopping. Real collectors don't want signs directing them to the Dusty Springfield section. They want to mooch around the aisles like treasure hunters. They don't know they're looking for Dusty Springfield until they see her, and begin to tingle.

Ken found the Geechie Wiley record in the drawer under the counter when he was looking for a magic marker. He set it by the cash register. At the end of the afternoon he carried it to the back of the store and dropped it into a box with a bunch of other records.

Dave didn't notice the record was missing for months.

One day he opened the drawer and it wasn't there. He couldn't remember the last time he had seen it.

He asked everyone who worked for him. They all swore they hadn't seen it, hadn't touched it. Dave didn't think of Ken for two days. "I tried to forget about him," he said to Brian.

When he finally tracked Ken down by phone, another month had passed.

"I remember that record," said Ken. "I filed it under Country."

"There isn't a Country section in the store," said Dave flatly. "I don't have a Country section." He was waving emphatically at the hundreds of signs hanging over the boxes of records. "There is no Country," he said.

When he hung up, he rubbed his eyes.

Brian was sitting beside him.

Dave said, "Where would you file a country record?"

"We don't have a Country section," said Brian.

"I know," said Dave. "But if you were filing a country record, where would you file it?"

"Depends," said Brian.

"On what?" said Dave.

"The artist," said Brian. "Living or dead?"

"Dead," said Dave.

"Accident or murder?" said Brian.

"I don't know," said Dave.

"Accident . . . I'd look under Skid Marks or the Never Fly at Night section. Murder I'd check, probably Surprise."

"What about natural causes?" said Dave.

"No one dies of natural causes in country music," said Brian.

Dave normally filed country records in one of two sections. They were the Grand Old Orgy and She Was So Sixteen. If it was hurting music he logged it under She Never Loved You Anyway.

Dave spent two days looking for Geechie Wiley. "What about Take This Jail and Shove It," said Brian helpfully, after they had looked everywhere they could think of.

"I've already checked," said Dave.

He never found a Country section.

"Well, I had one," said Ken, when Dave called him again. "It was near the back."

Dave looked for another day. Then he gave up.

"I keep thinking of that sleazebag from London," he said. "Do you remember him? He spent two days in here. He had a computer printout and a thick catalogue. He was smirking when he left. He was through the cash register at least ten times."

"Possible," said Brian. "But maybe it's still here."

They both looked out at the thousands of records.

"Maybe," said Dave.

That was seven years ago. Sam was only three years old the last time Dave had seen the Geechie Wiley record. Now Sam is in school—grade four. Any way you cut it, seven years is a long time. The seven-year itch, the seventh-inning stretch. They say every seven years your body replaces every single cell. After seven years there is nothing left of you.

Dave went through many stages with Geechie Wiley. First he blamed himself for leaving it lying around and sank into a pool of self-loathing. He was convinced a collector had spotted it and bought it when he wasn't in the store.

Then he decided that Ken, that fastidious little tidy-up clerk, knew all along what the record was worth and had swiped it when he fired him.

For a while he allowed himself to believe the record was still somewhere in the store, and that one day it would surface. As the months passed he thought of it less and less, wondering about it from time to time when he was alone and feeling wistful. But when he told the story of how it had slipped through his fingers, he was eventually able to tell it with humour, and these days when he told it, the joke was on him.

And now the kid had come back. And he was standing there in his blue suit and his yellow tie, and what was he saying? He was saying, "I can't believe your store is still here. Everything else has changed," he said. "But this place is exactly the same."

Dave looked around the store. He pointed to the lamp by the cash register.

"The lamp is new," he said. "I got that for my birthday, maybe three years ago."

"I remember that lamp," said Kevin. "You've had that lamp for at least seven years."

"We got rid of a lot of the eight-tracks," said Dave. "I don't buy eight-tracks any more. Except for the Partridge Family. Not that anyone is offering." The boy kept smiling as he looked around.

Seven years. He was a man now, not a boy. He said, "I'm not married any more. Do you remember Lisa? We got married. But it didn't work. She left. After three years. She said that I hadn't grown up. We didn't have kids. You have three, right?"

"Two," said Dave.

"You can make a living at this?" he said, waving his arm expansively around the store.

"Depends on what kind of living you want," said Dave, glancing at the cellphone Kevin had put down on the counter. He didn't finish the thought.

Kevin picked up the phone self-consciously and slipped it into his pocket. "For work," he said. Then he added, "I'm going to look around, okay?"

When he came back to the counter he was carrying five albums. *"Rock Lobster,"* he said holding a record up. *"Rock Lobster.* This might be the copy I sold you. I haven't heard this record for seven years."

"Do you still have a turntable?" said Dave.

"Somewhere," said Kevin. "Lisa took the CD player. I didn't buy a new one. I haven't had music for four years. Well, the radio."

"You had some nice records," said Dave. "I remember."

Kevin dropped *Rock Lobster* on the pile of records. "How much?" he asked.

"They're on the house," said Dave. "There's no charge."

It was blood money. Dave owed him for the Geechie Wiley. "I never gave you a wedding present. This is for the divorce. It's a starter set. You'll be back for more."

They both smiled.

"But this time," said Dave, "choose a girl who likes records. Okay?"

Dave walked with him to the front of the store. Kevin looked at his new records as they walked. Dave reached out and took his elbow to steer him around a milk crate.

Through the door Dave could see Emil, a neighbourhood street person, standing on the other side of the street, scratching his back awkwardly.

Dave said, "Wait a minute," and went back behind the counter.

Dave has always opposed giving Emil money. He and Morley have argued about this. "You give him money and he buys lottery tickets," says Dave. "You might as well throw the money away."

Dave slipped five twenties out of the cash register and slid them into an envelope. He turned around so Kevin couldn't see what he was doing. He sealed the envelope. The kid didn't need the money he owed him, but Dave had a debt to get rid of.

"See the old guy across the street," he said.

"Blue coat?" said Kevin. "Scratching?"

Dave held out the envelope. "Would you mind giving him this? Don't tell him where you got it."

Emil is crazy. In kinder times there would be a place for Emil. In these times there is the stairwell across from the record store. Mostly Emil inhabits a strange and unreachable world. Sometimes if someone says, "Hello, Emil," firmly enough they can pull him back from that world, and he will stop talking to himself and answer. Often he won't hear. Occasionally, he might spot people before they spot him. They are daydreaming, lost in their own world, and they walk by him without noticing, and Emil will call out, "HELLO," loudly and pointedly, leaving them wondering what the hell just happened.

That night, after he locked up, Dave walked across the street to see Emil. He was sitting on the sidewalk holding a wad of lottery tickets. Fifty, maybe more.

"What have you got there, Emil?" said Dave.

"Guy gave me a hundred dollars," he said, waving his handful of tickets. "I'm going to win the lottery. Again."

Dave stared at the tickets. Emil was so excited he hadn't recognized him. Dave turned to head home. "Good luck, Emil," he said. "Good luck."

The Bare Truth

*B*ert and Mary Turlington live in a spacious, semi-detached, brick house two doors away from Dave and Morley. They have been neighbours for twelve years. Although their children are different ages (Adam Turlington two years younger than Stephanie, the Turlington twins two years older than Sam) they have spent, if not a lot of time together, enough time—on the street, in each other's backyard, on various neighbourhood and school committees—to appreciate each other's neighbourly presence. They would not, under other circumstances, have become friends. But they are neighbours, and because they are neighbours, they have become friendly.

Bert Turlington is a criminal lawyer. Dave admires Bert's flippant self-confidence and enjoys the stories Bert loves to tell about his dodgy clients: Captain Hydroponic, the engineering student caught with two houses full of marijuana; Rudolph the Rastafarian, who spent his entire trial obsessively highlighting a battered copy of the Old Testament; and No-Neck Norman, part-time fence and full-time fink.

Bert had met No-Neck on the witness stand when the cops had brought him in to rat out one of Bert's clients. Bert had tried unsuccessfully to shake No-Neck's credibility for two and a half days.

"If I understand it right," said Bert to No-Neck, "you are a professional liar?"

"THAT'S RIGHT, COUNSELLOR," growled No-Neck proudly in his alcohol-ravaged rasp.

"And a professional thief?"

"THAT'S RIGHT, COUNSELLOR."

"He was such an ugly and appealing S.O.B. that I knew the jury believed every word he said," explained Bert. "In the end I convinced my client that the best we could do was cop a plea."

No-Neck had apparently enjoyed their courtroom sparring. A year later he showed up in Bert's office with a boxer who needed help.

"WONDER IF YOU NEED A CLIENT, COUNSELLOR?" he asked, handing Bert his business card. It read Labour Consultant.

Dave met No-Neck once—a heavy-set sixty-year-old, with a head the size of a pumpkin.

"They don't make them like Norman any more," said Bert ruefully.

It turned out Norman had tried, on any number of occasions, to retire from the world of crime, but apparently couldn't resist the easy money.

"Every time he gets into trouble," said Bert, "he bargains away the charges by ratting on someone or setting up a sting for the cops."

After a decade or so it got to the point that Norman had appeared on the stand one too many times. The police offered to put him in a witness-protection program, but they told him he would have to move to Alberta.

"Norman wouldn't hear of it," said Bert. "He told the cops he would rather be shot at home than move out west."

Bert Turlington was, in a sense, a tour guide, who led Dave into a world that he would otherwise never visit. Walking the dog with Bert was as good as going to Disneyland.

Once Bert took Dave to a boxing match in the ball-room of a fancy hotel. The room was crammed to the ceiling with eight hundred men—most of them wearing ill-fitting tuxedos and most of them smoking cigars they had bought from the table near the door where they were being freshly rolled by a Cuban woman not wearing any clothes. There were only two other woman in the room, both in scanty bathing suits—one selling cigarettes and the other holding up large numbered cards between each round.

"I'LL BET YOU DIDN'T THINK YOU COULD STILL BEHAVE LIKE THIS!" yelled Bert gleefully over the din as they settled into their ringside seats.

Another time when he went to dinner at the Turlingtons, Dave watched a loan shark drink an entire bottle of Scotch and fall headfirst into the chocolate mousse.

That was the night Mary put her foot down and told

Bert he couldn't bring clients home any more.

"It's not as much fun as it used to be," said Bert once. "There are more gun calls these days. And so much political correctness. The human element is going out of it. Everyone is so damn serious."

Bert likes to pace when he is planning his cases, and more than once, on warm summer nights when Dave has been out walking Arthur, he has bumped into Bert Turlington, and they have walked around the neighbourhood like a pair of long-distance truckers—Bert kicking at the sidewalk as he tries one argument after another on Dave, who plays the role of judge and jury.

Mary Turlington is a chartered accountant. Morley and Mary view the world from opposite ends of just about any spectrum you could imagine—except motherhood, a continuum of common ground that allows them to enjoy each other's company.

Dave and Mary, however, have not found a meeting ground. Dave thinks Mary is stiff. Mary thinks Dave is sanctimonious.

"He's a phoney," she said to Bert one Saturday morning as she cleared the breakfast dishes. "You watch . . . he'll be dressed like one of Adam's friends tonight. He'll be wearing a plaid shirt. Or something stupid."

Dave and Morley were coming to the Turlingtons' for dinner that night. Morley was going to be late. She had to be at the theatre early on.

"I could leave as soon as the curtain goes up," she had said when Mary had invited them. "I could be there soon after eight."

They had agreed Dave would go earlier—around six. But now that it was Saturday morning, the prospect of entertaining Dave for two long hours without the redeeming presence of his wife didn't seem like such a good idea any more. It was making Mary cranky.

"It's like he's still in college," she said. "The music. All that lah-dee-dah anti-bourgeois crap."

"I don't think he *went* to college," said Bert.

"Exactly," said Mary.

Mary Turlington grew up in London, Ontario, and went to the University of Western Ontario. She was accepted at McGill and Queen's but her family wasn't well off, and anyway, her father, who was working in construction at the time, didn't believe girls should go to university. Mary stayed at home and paid her own tuition. Thirty years later she was still anxious about money.

Money was why she became an accountant. When she was in high school her guidance counsellor had made her write down the stuff that she really loved. *You should do what you love,* he said. She wrote, "chocolate, *Columbo* on TV and books." She became an accountant so she would always have enough money for chocolate and books.

It hadn't turned out to be a bad choice. She liked the people she worked with. She liked the marble lobby and the gleaming windows of the office tower where she went every day. She liked the look of her business cards. After twenty-two years she had been made a partner in her firm—the first woman. She liked that. But if she was honest, if she was perfectly and completely honest, Mary would have to say that though she liked the order and comfort of numbers she didn't like the day-to-day business of doing her job.

But what else could she have done? Bookstores were going broke everywhere you looked. Books wouldn't have worked out. Right? *Right*.

And there was Dave, circling her life like an old lover—wandering down the street every morning in jeans and sneakers. Dave had turned *his* passion into a job. Why should his life be so easy?

Dave's antipathy towards Mary was more personal. He didn't like her politics. He didn't like her make-up. He didn't like the way she wore her hair. He didn't like the cracks she made about his record store. *How would you figure out the depreciation on an ABBA album, Dave?* As if he ran his store the way a doctor might run a hobby farm. As if it was nothing more than a tax write-off. Dave didn't know what the Turlingtons earned, but he figured he and Morley couldn't be *that* far behind.

At two o'clock that afternoon—Saturday afternoon— four hours before Dave was due to arrive, Mary Turlington was about to climb into the shower. She was standing in the bathroom squinting suspiciously at a bottle of Rain Forest Nut Meat! shampoo.

Bert poked his head into the bathroom and said he was going to get beer. Mary waved him away impatiently. She had three things on her mind: her hair, dinner and the pots and pans. She didn't have room for Bert and beer. She had bought some gunk advertised on television that was supposed to remove the rings from around the outside of her pots. She wanted to set her hair and then try the pot cleaner before she started cooking. And the shampoo. It was new too. She wanted to try it.

Mary has never liked her hair. Never. It is thin and brown and unless she fixes it, it hangs straight down, *like I have been buried for a week,* she is fond of saying.

When Mary was a girl, her mother taught her how to curl her hair using brown paper instead of curlers. Her mother ripped brown paper shopping bags into strips and while Mary's hair was still wet after washing, she would roll it into curls and tie the curls in place with the strips of brown paper. Mary would sleep with the paper in her hair and undo it in the morning.

When Mary went to university, her mother gave her a curling iron. Since she married Bert she has always been the first up—so she can fix her hair alone—a sacrosanct morning ritual that he interrupted only once.

The Nut Meat! shampoo must have been some kind of Third World joke. On the container was a promise that she would step out of the shower as if she were stepping out of a tropical rain forest, with a shiny head of lustrous hair cascading down her back. "Just shake it dry," read the instructions, "and the water droplets will bounce away like dew." When Mary stepped out of the shower and shook her head, her hair moved in a sodden, helmet-like clump. Like a head of matted felt. As if she had just shampooed with Elmer's glue.

"Damn," she said.

It was two-thirty. She was planning to serve paella. It was going to take her half an hour to untangle her hair. She wasn't going to have the time to clean the pots *and* get dinner ready. That didn't make her happy.

The thought of preparing the paella in front of Dave, who would probably sit at the kitchen table with a beer and yak at her while she cooked, the thought of Dave watching her make dinner in stained cookware propelled Mary into doing something she had never done in her life. She bolted out of the bathroom with nothing on and ran downstairs stark naked. Mary had never ever been downstairs with no clothes on. Never. Ever. It's not the sort of thing Mary Turlington does. But she was thinking that if she could get the gunk on the pots, they could season while she ran back upstairs and untangled her hair. And then she would be more or less back on schedule.

Bert and Mary have a galley kitchen. It is small by any standards and cut off from the rest of the house by an island counter. You have to go through the family room to get to the kitchen, through the family room and past the sliding glass doors that lead to the patio, past the table where the Turlingtons eat most of their meals, past the island counter and then you are there, in Mary's kitchen, which is not unlike being in a dead-end alley.

Mary flew naked by the patio door without even considering that someone could see her from outside. She *was* alone after all. Bert was getting beer. The twins were at a movie. God knows where Adam was. Then she began pulling all the pots and pans out of the pot cupboard, moving so fast she didn't even notice what it felt like to be nude in the kitchen.

It hardly took her a minute to get all the pots and pans arranged upside down on the counter in front of her. She was squinting at the instructions on the spray when someone knocked on the patio door.

This can't be happening, she thought.

Actually she didn't really think anything. She gasped and leapt back a good three feet, launching the can of cleaner across the kitchen. She came down in a crouch, alarmingly aware that *she wasn't wearing any clothes!*

One summer night soon after they were married, Bert had taken Mary to his family's cottage for a week. He had talked her into going skinny-dipping. It had felt surprisingly exotic, the water cool and flawless on her skin, her body strong and liberated.

This didn't feel anything like that. This felt like a chilly breeze moving along her backside, this felt like the hairs on her arms sticking up, like an unpleasant prickling that seemed to be centred around her waist and was spreading up her spine. Her skin felt tight. And cold.

Whoever it was knocked again.

Mary looked desperately around for something to cover herself. The only thing she could see was a tea towel hanging on the handle of the stove. She reached out, snatched it and held it in front of her . . . her what? It seemed no bigger than a handkerchief. First up and then down. The tea towel clearly wasn't up to the job. Her heart was racing. *Don't panic,* she thought as she backed into a corner of the kitchen, panicking, waving the towel in front of her like a bullfighter. Like something pathetic from the Playboy Channel. *Don't panic.* Whoever was knocking couldn't see her from the door. If she didn't do anything, surely they would go away.

There was a silent moment that seemed to stretch forever. Mary barely breathed. Maybe they had given up. Maybe they had gone away.

And then, whoever was knocking slid the screen open and knocked on the glass. Mary hid behind the only thing available. Her knees.

Then the glass door slid open.

And Mary draped the tea towel over her head.

"Hello," said a voice. "Is anyone home?"

It was Dave.

Who else?

If she didn't move, surely he would go away.

"Hello," said Dave louder, stepping into the family room.

"Yo, Dave." It was Bert, coming up the basement stairs. *Back from the beer store already?*

Mary was not at this moment acting rationally. She

knew only two things: she was nude, and soon she would be surrounded by men. When the glass door slid open, she had moved beyond rational thought into a world of primal instincts.

Her instinct told her there was one thing to do and that was *to get out of sight!* Sadly there was no way out of the kitchen without passing Dave. That left one place to go. And so, with lizard-like agility, that's where Mary went—headfirst into the cupboard she had just emptied of pots.

The cupboard was directly under the countertop stove. It was not much larger than a dishwasher. It had two doors separated by a four-inch wooden post. Mary snaked around the post and folded herself up like a croissant. There was one shelf—it had always annoyed her because it wasn't nailed down, and it rattled whenever she removed a pot. If it hadn't been loose she would not have fitted. She wouldn't have fitted under normal circumstances. She was carried into the cupboard on the wave of her anxiety. She lay there, in the fetal position, with her back pressed against one wall and her feet pressing against the other. Her knees pushing into her chest. Her face smushed against the cupboard door.

Dave was standing only a few feet away.

"No one is home at my place," he was saying. "I've locked myself out. I'm not sure if you guys still have a key."

"It's in the dining-room cupboard," said Mary desperately under her breath.

"I don't think so," said Bert. "But I'll ask Mary. She'll know."

"The dining-room cupboard, you idiot," hissed Mary.

She tried to will her husband to the dining room.

Bert disappeared. He returned almost immediately. "I thought she was upstairs," he said. "She must have gone to pick stuff up for dinner. I was just going to fix some lunch. Are you hungry? I can make you an omelette."

Then he said, "I wonder why she has all the pots out like this?"

He is going to open the cupboard, thought Mary. *He is going to open the cupboard to check if there are any pots left.*

What, she thought, *is going to happen when he reaches into the cupboard looking for a pan and comes up with a handful of his wife? What would he think had been going on? Walking into his house and finding his neighbour standing in his kitchen and his naked wife stuffed into the cupboard.*

If he opened the door she was going to have to act fast.

She decided she would jump out, yell *Surprise!* and let the chips fall where they may. It was the best she could think of.

But Bert didn't open the cupboard.

He turned on the stove.

It took about a minute for the cupboard to start heating up.

Mary is slightly claustrophobic at the best of times. She gets anxious when the subway stops inexplicably between stations; when elevators seem to have arrived at the floor but the doors don't open; when the power goes off and everything is so black you can't see your hand.

She couldn't see her hand now and she was starting to get anxious. She felt as if something was sitting on her chest. She could feel her heart beating rapidly, feel the moths beginning to flutter around her stomach. She could also feel her leg going to sleep.

In the kitchen Bert was not only making an omelette, he was mixing juice and fixing a salad. She heard the fridge door swing open and a little exclamation of joy puncture the kitchen.

"Whoa! Look at this," he said. "You want an olive?"

Mary opened the cupboard door a crack so she could see too. Bert was holding out the plate of antipasto she had prepared for supper.

"We shouldn't eat much of this," said Bert. "Spread it around a bit so the boss won't notice."

The boss? The boss????

The idiots were trying to rearrange her salad plate to cover their footprints. Mary almost crawled out then and there. She imagined herself appearing in front of them as naked as truth itself, *"Won't notice? Won't notice? . . . I notice everything."*

But then what? Walk upstairs? Crawl back into the cupboard?

Her leg was beginning to cramp. Now it was starting

to twitch. She thought of what happened to their dog's
back leg when you scratched its belly. It felt as if her leg
was going to start banging away like the dog's at any
moment.

Damn. If she started to thump away like that—as if
she was out of control—and Bert opened the door and
found her.

Ohmigod, she thought.

A half-hour passed. Forty-five minutes. The
omelette was eaten and forgotten. She had been in
there an hour and fifteen minutes. She felt as if she had
been canned. It was like a steam bath. She was afraid
she might be running out of air.

Dave and Bert were still sitting at the table—
picking at a cheesecake that was supposed to be for
dessert.

Bert said, "I was supposed to get beer. Do you want
to come? Or you can stay. The Canadian Tire catalogue
just came. You can stay and check it out if you want."

Mary didn't hear what Dave decided.

She heard the patio door open and close. Then she
heard nothing. A deep and dead silence. She opened
the door a few inches and light and cool air flooded in.
She couldn't see anyone or anything. She decided to
wait for a few moments.

Even if she had checked, even if she had opened the
door completely, she wouldn't have seen Dave
slouched on the couch in the family room staring
morosely at the Canadian Tire catalogue. The island
counter blocked him from her view. He turned a few

pages absentmindedly. He looked at his wrist and up at the phone on the wall. Twenty-five minutes had passed since he had last called home.

He stood up and walked across the family room to the small white desk beside the phone. There were cubbyholes on the wall above the desk, each one carefully labelled: Bills to Pay, Filing, School Notices, Pay Stubs. *Just like Mary Turlington,* he thought, *every piece of paper obsessively organized.*

Dave's eyes widened. There was an envelope in the slot marked Pay Stubs. Reddick and Rowe. The accountancy firm where Mary worked. He reached out and slid the envelope up an inch and a half. It had been slit open. He could see through the little window that there was still a cheque, or at least a cheque stub, inside.

He dropped the envelope back in place. He would have left it there if it had been Bert's cheque. But it was Mary's cheque. And Mary had made him feel like a child for too long. She might not have said it straight out, but Mary had made it all too clear that his involvement with rock and roll precluded him from the world of adults. Yet he knew that if he was an executive with some major record label she wouldn't find him childish. He suspected that Mary would be tickled to have Bruce Springsteen as a neighbour, would be delighted to have Sting over for supper. So it wasn't about music. It was about *money*. Well, how much did *she* think was enough? How much was *she* being paid to live her grown-up life?

The answer was in his hand.

He turned the envelope over and pulled the pay stub out. Upside down.

Something startled him. There was a noise, a breath, something he didn't quite hear, something he sensed more than he heard, more of a presence than a sound. Something that told him he wasn't alone. He felt as if he was being watched. He whirled around and for the briefest moment locked eyes with Mary.

Ohmigod, he thought. *Ohmigod. Ohmigod. Ohmigod.*

She was standing on the far side of the kitchen counter.

He looked down at the envelope he was holding and then back across the counter.

She has seen me, he was thinking, the sickening sense of being caught descending upon him like a fog. He was only dimly aware that there was something peculiar about the way she looked.

But she wasn't there any more. She had vanished— a pink blur, gone so fast that Dave couldn't be sure about what he had seen. He dropped the pay stub back in the slot and sat down on the couch. There was a brief sense of reprieve, then there was humiliation, embarrassment, confusion.

He went home, not sure whether he could ever come back.

Mary didn't reappear until Bert returned with the beer. Soon after Bert came home, she wandered downstairs in her Alfred Sung separates, wearing a string of pearls and looking her normally sophisticated self. The zipper on the back of the skirt, however, was not zipped completely shut. And Bert had to tuck in the label of her top, which was sticking out in a most un-Mary-like way.

There was an odd air to the dinner that night. A vague undercurrent of something that Morley tried to quantify as she and Dave walked home.

She started with Mary's hair.

"What did you think of it?" she asked Dave.

"What?" said Dave.

"It was pretty high fashion," said Morley. "All stiff and swept over to one side. Like it was glued or something."

"I didn't notice," said Dave.

Mary had drunk more than usual.

"Did you see the look Bert gave her when she opened the last bottle of wine?"

Dave shook his head. Grunted noncommittally.

Morley kept going as she unlocked the front door.

"There was *something* going on. I don't know. Do you think they're having a hard time?"

Dave shrugged. "I dunno," he said.

He had barely looked at Mary all night, his eyes skittering away from her whenever he talked. When Bert brought up provincial politics, Dave began an anti-government tirade but petered out almost immediately. When they started talking about his record store Dave braced himself for the requisite quip from Mary, but nothing came.

"You and Mary usually squabble about something," said Morley. "Maybe you two are mellowing out or something."

"Maybe," said Dave. He was heading up the stairs.

"Do you think you could bear to see more of them?"

Dave stopped halfway up the stairs. "I think we've seen enough of each other for now," he said.

Susan Is Serious

*I*n January, Morley received *a letter* from Calgary, from a university friend she hadn't spoken to in over ten years. It was a breezy note full of family news, about her daughter and her dog, about hair dye and hot flashes, as if they had never stopped talking. As if they were still sitting up all night. Four pages. Handwritten.

We are coming to town in February, it ended. *Matthew is getting an award from Junior Achievement— Enterprise in Action. We should get together. It would be so good to see you. Love, Susan.*

Morley wrote back that night. *Why don't you stay with us?*

It never occurred to her that Susan would accept.

Though she wasn't unhappy when she did.

Morley was *delighted* about the prospect of seeing Susan again.

And her kids.

Especially her kids.

Morley had never met Susan's children. Imagine— the two of them with kids. Husbands. Pets. Home and School. Moms. *Sheesh.* Morley was *excited* about the visit.

Morley and Susan shared a house in their last two years of university—the Bird House. Six bedrooms—seven girls. Colleen slept in what should have been the living room. She swore she could hear rats moving around the basement at night.

There were enough memories in those years to last a lifetime. Morley would have welcomed any of those women into her house without a second thought.

Even that old guinea hen Harriet Swerdkoff.

But here comes Susan—the organized one.

Morley had lingered over Susan's letter when she finished reading it. Her handwriting hadn't changed. The letters still big and round. The *i*'s still dotted with circles.

When you missed a class it was Susan's notes you borrowed.

Susan the duck. Susan who tried a little harder than anyone else. Susan whose room was a little neater. Susan who was a little more responsible, a little more . . . uptight?

Well, maybe.

But at a time when everyone else was confused about the future, Susan always knew exactly what she wanted.

Susan who had a subscription to both *Bride's Own* and *The Economist*.

Susan. And Susan's kids. A fifteen-year-old daughter. And Matthew, the twelve-year-old Junior Achiever.

They arrived on a Tuesday afternoon. Took a taxi from the airport. A limo, actually.

"Is she a rock star?" whispered Sam, when he saw the sleek car idling at the curb.

The only other time anyone had arrived at their house in a limousine it was Mark Knofler, on his way to a concert in Buffalo, diverted to Toronto during a snowstorm. He spent the night with them—driftwood from Dave's past life.

"No," said Morley. "A friend. She's an old friend."

Susan emerged from the limo in designer jeans and a brown suede jacket. She looked back over her shoulder, waiting for her daughter, before she strode up Morley's front walk. Her green leather purse matched her green leather shoes. Her deep red lipstick matched her deep red nails. She was wearing a stylish gold chain.

Morley was waiting at the door, running her hand through her hair, seeing herself through Susan's eyes. It was not a pretty sight—Birkenstocks, jeans (worn through at the knee), one of Dave's old shirts.

"Come in. Come in!" Morley shouted. But that's not what she was thinking. She was thinking, *Damn it. Damn it.*

"Susan," she said, her arms wide. Then she said, "You must be Matthew."

The boy took off a pair of sunglasses—tortoise-shell—and slipped them into a glasses case.

"Pleased to meet you," he said, holding out his hand, smiling, making eye contact. A firm shake. A Junior Achiever shake.

"Sam," said Morley. She had to turn around to find him. Sam had begun to back away from the door.

"Sam!" said Morley, pushing him forward, "this is Matthew."

Out snapped Matthew's hand. Sam looked down at it in confusion, then back at his mother. Matthew's hand continued to hover in the air between them. Sam had never shaken hands with someone his age. He knew what he was expected to do. But it felt *wrong*. He started to back away again. He caught Morley's frown, stopped, said, "HI?" and waved his arm vaguely in the direction of this boy.

"Pleased to meet you, *Sam!*" said Matthew.

Sam looked back at his mother.

"Why don't you two go downstairs," she said.

Matthew took off his shoes and set them neatly by the door.

Morley turned to the girl. Jennifer. Fifteen. Jennifer was wearing blue jeans. Rolled at the ankle so you could see her socks.

White.

The jeans had been ironed—there was a crease running down the front. Jennifer's hair was short, in the fashion of the 1920s. And neat. Maybe even sprayed neat. She was wearing three hair clips. One in the front and two on either side—each one carefully positioned to restrain rogue hairs that might make a break.

"And you must be . . . Jennifer," said Morley.

All this was happening very quickly.

The daughter, Jennifer, stepped forward and stuck out *her* hand. Like her brother, she looked Morley straight in the eye. It was a confidence belied by the way she shifted her weight uncomfortably from one foot to the other. They shook hands. A moment later Jennifer was in the living room, her backpack open at her feet. She was examining her hair in a hand-held mirror, as if the act of shaking hands might have knocked something out of place—patting the top of her head the way a mechanic would pat the hood of a troublesome, but favourite, car.

Ten minutes later Morley and Susan were in the kitchen.

"Are you still married to the dentist?" asked Morley. She was fixing coffee.

"Orthodontist," said Susan.

"Bruce," said Morley.

"Brian," said Susan.

That's right. Brian.

Susan had begun dating Brian at the end of their graduating year. It was coming back. He was an athlete. Football? Or swim team? Almost went to the Olympics. Or something. Morley couldn't remember his face. She tried, but all that came back was the vague smell of chlorine.

"The swimmer," ventured Morley. "Right?"

"Diver," said Susan. "He almost went to the Olympics."

"Right," said Morley.

Susan was fiddling with her wedding ring. Taking it off, putting it on. Twisting it around and around. Morley took a sip of her coffee and remembered the rainy Saturday afternoon the two of them had sat on the floor in Susan's bedroom with Susan's monumental collection of bridal magazines piled around them. They had spent the afternoon designing their ultimate wedding. Morley thought they were goofing around, until she realized that Susan was serious— Susan was making plans.

Upstairs, Sam was sitting on his bed, watching Matthew unpack. He stared with fascination as Matthew lined his toiletries in order, by height, along the window ledge: a bottle of vitamins, a bottle of Tommy Hilfiger cologne, plastic bottles of shampoo and conditioner, a hairbrush, a toothbrush. When Matthew was satisfied with the way they looked, he turned his attention to his clothes, which he arranged in the corner on the floor as carefully as if he was arranging a window display for a fancy men's store— an island of calm amid the storm of Sam's bedroom.

When he was finished, he stood up and smiled at Sam. "That feels better," he said. Then he reached into his briefcase and pulled out a thick blue binder with the Junior Achiever crest stamped on the cover.

"Do you want to see my business plan?" he asked.

Next door, Jennifer was sitting on Stephanie's bed, watching Stephanie root through a pile of clothes, a pile on the floor of her bedroom that began at the door and was almost level with the mattress by the time it reached her bed. Stephanie was looking for lip gloss.

"I know it's here somewhere," she said.

"Don't you have to make your bed in the morning?" asked Jennifer, looking around the room with what was clearly admiration.

"*What*?" said Stephanie. She was peering with satisfaction at a CD that had dropped out of a handful of dirty laundry.

"I've been looking for this for weeks," she said.

Downstairs, Dave was sitting at the kitchen table reading the paper when something distracted him. He looked up, not sure what was tugging at his attention. Then he frowned. It was perfume. He turned and there was Matthew, standing not three feet away, staring at the back of his head. Or was it the paper? He was staring at the paper.

"Would you like some of the paper?" asked Dave.

"Could I please look at the business section?" asked Matthew.

This must be what small towns are like, thought Morley later, as the kids arrived in pairs for dinner— everyone struggling to fit around the too-small kitchen table, Dave helping her carry dishes back and forth from the stove. She was happy. There is something lovely about seeing your children paired up with the children of your old friends. The chaos reminded her of dinners at the Bird House.

Halfway through the first course, Matthew put down his knife and fork, looked around and said,

"These are delicious mashed potatoes."

Morley caught Sam rolling his eyes at Stephanie.

She threw him daggers. Then she smiled at Matthew.

"Thank you, Matthew," she said.

Morley had, during the three brief hours since they arrived, become painfully aware that there was a chasm separating her children and Susan's children. Susan's children, it would seem, had manners, as if they had been raised by humans. Sam and Stephanie, on the other hand, seemed to have been raised by wolves. *Look at them,* thought Morley, *slouched in front of their plates, smacking and snorting, wiping their greasy paws on their fur.*

Later that night when they are alone in their bedroom Dave will shake his head and say, "That is one weird kid."

He'll be talking about Matthew.

"I don't think he even *liked* those mashed potatoes," Dave will say. "He didn't even finish his mashed potatoes."

"Those were manners, Dave," Morley will say. "In case you didn't notice."

"'These are delicious mashed potatoes.' Jeez! Come on, Morley. It's the sort of thing you'd do if you were eating dinner at your boss's house. He's twelve. He's twelve years old." He will almost tell Morley about Matthew's business card, but before he does, he will notice the way she is looking at him, and he won't say any more.

But that is later . . .

Now they are still at the table . . . eating.

And in that moment after Matthew had said, "These are delicious mashed potatoes," and Morley had frowned at Sam because he was rolling his eyes at Stephanie, a silence settled on the dinner table. All you could hear was the rattle of cutlery, as if *everyone* was enjoying the potatoes.

But the silence lasted a beat too long and abruptly deepened and became a tomb-like silence, so no one was listening to the cutlery any more but to the silence itself—a silence that was spiralling deeper by the second. Morley was desperately trying to think of something to say, something to get them out of the silence before it was too late, imploring Dave with her eyes for help. *Say something!*

Everyone was thinking the same thing now—the whole table bound together in silent agony, everyone struggling against the surface viscosity of the silence, like a table full of water bugs squirting around a dark pond, like a table of slow-motion scuba divers floating away on a deadly current of silence.

It was finally Sam who put down his cutlery with a flourish. And everyone thought, *Thank God,* turning and looking at him with relief and expectation and great hope.

Sam smiled at them all and said, "You know what really *pisses me off?*"

Morley saw Susan clutch her knife and fork, and watched her check her children's reactions: Matthew,

his brow furrowed—puzzled; Jennifer staring at Sam
with a mixture of awe, respect, disbelief . . . and
ohmigod . . . approval!

Not twenty minutes later, just when she thought
things couldn't get worse, Morley caught Susan
frowning at the floor by the stove. Morley followed
her eyes to the crack between the stove and the
kitchen counter and saw what had caught Susan's
attention, a forgotten Roach Motel, lying there like a
pile of dirty laundry.

An hour later Morley came into the kitchen to fill her
coffee cup and Susan was wiping the counter with a
sponge. Susan looked up and smiled self-consciously.

"I was just wiping the counter," she said unneces-
sarily.

They both stared at the sponge awkwardly and then
back at each other. Both remembering that twenty-five
years ago, when they lived together, everyone always
knew Susan was upset when she began to clean
compulsively.

The next night Stephanie came bouncing down the
stairs when she was called to dinner, but there was no
Jennifer.

"Where's Jennifer?" asked Morley.

"I lent her one of my tops," said Stephanie. "She's
getting changed."

When Jennifer came downstairs she was wearing
Stephanie's yellow lip gloss and a matching yellow
halter top. She dropped into her seat and arched her

back coyly, which made the tank top inch up her midriff, exposing her navel.

No one said anything.

Jennifer picked up her fork, looked around the silent table and said, "You know what really pisses *me* off?"

Susan picked up a napkin and started to polish her spoon.

After dinner Morley walked into the kitchen, and Susan was standing by the sink with her hands behind her back. Morley pretended not to see the can of cleanser Susan was hiding. She had been washing the table.

Susan left the next afternoon. Two days early.

"I decided we should visit their grandparents for a few days," said Susan.

They both knew that wasn't true. Oh, they *were* going to stay with their grandparents, all right. But *not* because Susan thought a visit would be nice. The truth was Susan couldn't get Jennifer away from Sam and Stephanie fast enough.

After they left, Morley sat on the stairs and had a good cry. The aborted visit had rattled her. Things that she thought she loved looked shoddy now that she was looking at them through Susan's eyes. The jukebox in the living room looked . . . juvenile.

The house looked . . . dirty.

She scooped up a dust ball from behind a chair and stuck it in her pocket as she wandered into the kitchen. The breakfast dishes were still not done. Arthur the dog was sitting in a chair licking a sticky half-full bowl of pinkish cereal milk someone had left on the table.

Morley thought of the house that she grew up in. Bathrooms that never seemed to get dirty. The smell of furniture polish and lemon cleanser. Ironed sheets folded neatly in orderly cupboards. The comfortable warmth of home baking.

When she began to measure her house against her mother's house, Morley felt like a failure. She thought she had been running a casual, comfortable house. She was abruptly aware that she had been neglecting the wider implications. She'd been raising a herd of slobs.

After dinner she sat everyone down.

"There are going to be some changes around here," she said.

Beds had to be made before anyone went to school.

Sam would wash dishes after supper.

Stephanie was in charge of the upstairs bathroom.

Dave avoided looking at Morley during her speech. Sam and Stephanie both opened their mouths at the same time, but neither got a word out.

"No allowance," said Morley. "No allowance if your chores aren't done. And done properly."

That was January.

Everything went surprisingly well for a week or two.

More or less. As okay as these things go. Well, they didn't really go okay at all. Things were actually rather unpleasant.

Every morning began with a fight over the beds. They were made, every morning. More or less. The way beds get made under these kinds of circumstances.

After about two weeks the alarm rang one morning and Dave opened a weary eye and proclaimed the arrival of the day like a ring announcer proclaiming the beginning of a prizefight. "Oh good, it's morning again," he began. "And this morning we have, in the south bedroom, with allowance in her pocket and determination in her heart . . . Mom. And in the back bedroom, twisted in sheets that haven't been washed in weeks, months, years . . . a ten-year-old boy. Let the fun begin. What is this? Round twelve?" He got out of bed and slouched into the bathroom. That's how things were going.

In the middle of week three, Sam, who was supposed to be washing the dinner dishes each night, took his allowance to the Biway and came back with a huge package of paper plates and three boxes of plastic cutlery.

That night he came into the kitchen while Morley was cooking so he could monitor the number of dishes she used.

"Why do you need another pot?"

"You don't need a new spoon for the gravy. Use the spoon from the peas."

Stephanie started to patrol the bathrooms—refusing one night to let Dave use the one by the bedrooms. She stood in front of it, her arms across the door.

"I just cleaned this one. He can use the one down-stairs. He's too lazy to go downstairs."

One morning Stephanie went to leave the house without making her bed.

Morley said, "You are not going to school until your bed is made."

They stood in the hall glaring at each other, nose to nose. Neither of them about to give way, until a dim light began to shine in the back of Stephanie's eyes—an idea was approaching, like a train coming from far away in the night. Morley saw it coming and thought, *Oh no,* but what could she do?

You are not going to school until your bed is made.

"Fine," said Stephanie. She went back into her bedroom and slammed the door behind her. Morley stared at the closed door and thought, *Now what do I do?*

It was not a happy home.

But it was cleaner and it was neater. And that was good enough for Morley. That is what she wanted.

A month after Susan left, Morley's mother, Helen, came over for dinner. The plan was for Helen to eat dinner, then sleep over Friday night. When Morley went to pick her mother up, she thought how nice it was going to be to have someone in the house who would share her point of view—someone who would approve of the changes. Morley had told Helen what was going on—about her plans to organize the house. She was sure Helen would be delighted.

But on Saturday morning Helen seemed agitated. Instead of sitting at the kitchen table reading bits of the newspaper out loud to whomever happened by, Helen was suddenly anxious to help out. Each time Morley came into the kitchen with a load of laundry, a rag or a dirty plate, Helen kept pushing the paper aside and struggling up.

"Can I help?" she kept asking.

Morley didn't understand what was going on at first. Helen normally loved to sit at the table and read the minutiae of the nation out loud to anyone who wandered by. Having Helen over for breakfast was like eating with CNN, and Morley couldn't figure out why the visit was going so badly. She almost snapped at her mother once, but she bit her tongue. Just before lunch she finally realized her mother wasn't going to relax until everyone else did. She wanted to be a part of whatever was going on. Morley went into the kitchen with a can of polish and asked Helen if she would like to help dust the den.

Helen looked up at her, irritation clouding her face.

"I was just reading the book reviews," she snapped.

Later, after she had dropped her mother home, Morley drove across the city, alone, listening to the radio, remembering another night years ago, when she had also been in the car alone. It was not long after her father, Roy, had died. She was worried about Helen. She had driven out of her way to knock on her mother's door.

Helen had been sitting in the living room reading. Morley had seen the book open on the chair by the window. But what had caught Morley's eye wasn't the book, but the wooden tray with Helen's dinner dishes still in front of the television. Morley couldn't believe her eyes. Couldn't believe that her mother had let the dishes sit while she sat and read. It was a small thing but it was completely out of character. It wasn't something she thought Helen was capable of doing.

"I am worried about her, Dave," said Morley when she came home that night.

Her mother, who had been so neat and so perfect all her life, would never have let the dishes sit around like that when her husband was alive. Roy was a policeman. His basement workshop was as clean as Helen's kitchen. His garden tool shed was as tidy as her cupboards. Roy liked things orderly and precise. What would Roy have thought of those dishes?

It was Dave who said, "Maybe that's the point."

Morley didn't get it. She had fretted for a week, worried that her mother was coming unglued. Worried she was losing it. She called her every day—sometimes twice a day. And then one afternoon, on her way up from the basement, she understood. Understood that the small and insignificant act of leaving those dishes unwashed was an act of letting go. An act of healing. Helen had spent her whole life keeping her house perfect because that's what *Roy* had wanted. All those perfect beds, all those spotless counters were in deference to her husband. Now she was living alone. She wasn't about to live like a slob, but she wasn't going to worry so much any more either. It was a liberating insight.

Those dirty dishes left in front of the television turned out to be a gift to Morley. They had given her permission to run her house her own way, and now years later Morley was aware that the way she had been running her house was a conscious choice—a choice she had made paying attention to the lessons of her mother's life. Morley realized that Helen didn't just approve, she *liked* Morley's house. She liked the jukebox in the living room. She liked her grandchildren. She felt comfortable with the way Morley and Dave were bringing them up. They might not be collecting Junior Achievement awards, but they did have standards. Different from Susan's certainly, but so what?

Morley didn't put any cutlery on the table that night. "Caveman," she said. "Caveman dinner."

"How am I supposed to eat mashed potatoes without a fork?" said Stephanie.

"Like this," said Sam, dipping his fingers into his potatoes. Smacking his furry little paws clean.

"You're disgusting, Sam," said Stephanie.

And just like that things returned to normal.

Of course things never really return to normal. Two weeks after the caveman supper—two months after Susan's disastrous visit—Morley got up one morning to find Sam already up and dressed. When she walked into his room to wake him, he was making his bed.

She was about to say something, but she bit her tongue. Instead, she said, "It is a lovely morning out. I think, no jacket. When you're finished, we'll make pancakes."

Sam was oblivious. He was struggling with his bed, his brow furrowed in concentration.

"How do you do the tight corners?" he asked. "I've *always* liked to make *my* bed with tight corners."

Morley shook her head in sympathy.

"It's tricky," she said, reaching for the sheet.

I FALL TO PIECES

Odd Jobs

It was on a Saturday afternoon in September, five years ago, that Dave and Morley sat in their backyard and had one of those conversations that married couples have from time to time, about where they had been and where they were going. It was during that conversation that they decided, once again, that they would, without fail, start saving money. They agreed to put away two hundred dollars a month in an account they would never touch, never, not ever. And for the last five years they have been doing that, making those monthly deposits—to their own amazement, without missing one month. They did, however, miss one step because it seemed so self-evident, they never hammered out *why* they were saving. This was not a problem when they were beginning and there was no money in the account, but after five years Dave and Morley had accumulated a significant nest egg, and nest eggs have a habit of hatching.

What had hatched in Dave's mind was a duck-egg-blue 1969 Austin-Healey 3000, with a cream scallop inlet, a red leather interior, fifty-two-spoke wire wheels and Lucas fog lights mounted on a shiny chrome bar.

Ted Bescher, a retired schoolteacher who lives across the lane from Dave and Morley, owns a bright yellow TR6 that Dave has admired ever since Ted, and his car, moved into the neighbourhood. Ted's car hardly ever leaves the garage, but it is there calling out to Dave whenever he walks by. And sometime after his forty-fifth birthday Dave realized that under certain circumstances, just to be able to say that you owned an Austin-Healey would make your world a better place. He wouldn't *have* to drive it. In fact, he wasn't entirely sure he *could* drive an Austin-Healey without worrying what people were saying behind his back. But just to have one in his garage would make life better.

Morley, of course, had *her* own plans for the money, which had nothing to do with little blue cars. When Morley thought about the savings account she imagined a new second-floor bathroom, where there would always be clean towels and a dry toilet seat.

These were not things they talked about, however, until one summer morning when they were eating breakfast, and Morley looked at the toaster and said, "It would work so much better if we could plug it in at the table. So we wouldn't have to get up and walk across the kitchen every time someone wanted toast."

It was just an idle thought, but it struck her as a good one. She considered it for a moment and said, "Maybe we should take some of the money from the savings account and get someone to put in another outlet."

This sent a chill through Dave's heart.

The next morning, a Saturday morning, Dave was sitting alone at the breakfast table looking at the toaster on the other side of the kitchen. He was thinking, *I should install the outlet myself.* It had nothing to do with toast. It was a defensive manoeuvre. It had everything to do with the Austin-Healey.

Morley was already at work—they were opening a new play. As she left, she said she wouldn't be back until after the curtain came down.

The kids were still asleep—Dave wouldn't see *them* for hours. Sometime in July their body clocks had slipped into the Pacific time zone. Dave had the whole day stretched out before him like a white line running down the centre of a highway. How complicated could it be for an old roadie to run some wires through a wall and install an outlet?

The more he thought about it the more he liked the idea. What he liked best of all was that he would get to knock holes in the kitchen wall. It felt good just *thinking* about that. Without thinking about it any further, without letting coffee or the morning paper waylay him, Dave fetched a hammer from the basement. He returned to the kitchen and stared at the bare white wall beside the table, tapping the hammer anxiously on his thigh.

Like a Spanish conquistador sealing the fate of his troops by burning his ship as soon his last man stepped on shore, Dave raised the hammer over his head and swung it at the wall with all his might. *Hiii-yah.*

The hammer sank into the plaster with a pleasing crack. Dave pulled it out. *Take no prisoners! No turning back!* Three more whacks, and he was staring at a hole the size of a cantaloupe.

What a glorious feeling of destructive accomplishment. Not as good perhaps as changing the oil of a small blue Austin-Healey, but good nevertheless. Dave gave the edges of his hole a few prods with the butt of the hammer and bits of plaster flaked onto the floor. Then he reluctantly put the hammer down. He went upstairs to look for the big *Reader's Digest Book of Home Repairs* to see where he should find the wire that he was going to run to his hole. To his new outlet. It would have to come from somewhere.

He rooted around the bedroom for a while and decided he must have lent the book to a neighbour. He went downstairs and stared at his hole and decided to clean it up a bit. By the time he had finished tinkering, the hole was more symmetrical, neater and considerably larger. More the size of a pizza than a melon. A largish pizza, thought Dave.

He wondered if Jim Scoffield had his repair book. He didn't really need it, but it would be good to see what the *Reader's Digest* had to say before he went too far. He glanced at the kitchen clock. Jim was the kind of neighbour you visited rather than phoned.

"I don't have your book," said Jim, "but I have a new mallet. I can't believe you started without me. Let me get it."

Jim and Dave stared at the hole where Dave wanted to put the new outlet.

"Where's the wire going to come from?" asked Jim.

"That's what I was wondering," said Dave.

Jim pointed at a light switch by the back door. "There'd be wire over there we could patch into," he said.

Then he smiled. "Of course, we'll have to punch a hole in the wall to pick it up."

He was fiddling with his new mallet.

"Be my guest," said Dave.

"Are you sure?" said Jim, moving towards the back wall, not waiting for the answer.

Two satisfying swings and Jim was through the plaster. Dave pushed forward to peer into the hole. Jim pushed him back. "Maybe," said Jim, "I should tidy that up a bit."

There *were* wires there. In fact, when Jim stepped back and they both peeked in his hole, wires were about all they *could* see—all sorts of wires. Black shiny wires, grey cloth-covered wires, wires snaking through the wall like . . .

"Like spaghetti," said Jim.

"We're not wanting for wire," said Dave.

Jim pointed at a grey wire running through a porcelain insulator.

"Knob and tube," said Jim. "I didn't think that stuff was legal any more."

"Those aren't live," said Dave. "I had an electrician in to replace all that a couple of years ago."

Dave reached into the hole with his screwdriver and jiggled the old wire. There was a sudden puff of smoke. Dave gasped and the right side of his body jerked spastically. A deep alien-like moan rolled out of him as the screwdriver flew across the kitchen, end over end like a tomahawk, ricocheting off the kitchen sink and disappearing through the window.

There was a moment of stunned silence. Jim and Dave both stared at the broken window as shards of glass tinkled to the floor.

"Could you do that again?" said Jim. "I especially enjoyed the way the chip of porcelain from the sink followed the screwdriver through the window."

A minute later Bert Turlington was standing on the stoop. He had Dave's screwdriver in his hand. "This yours?" he asked, standing a little close, talking a little loud.

Dave nodded. Yes.

"Are you out of your mind?" said Bert, even louder now.

Dave shrugged his shoulders. No.

"I opened the back door," said Bert, "and this is flying across my yard like . . ."

"A tomahawk?" said Dave helpfully.

"It stuck in the door frame about a foot from my head," said Bert.

"We're moving some wires," said Dave. "I got a shock."

"You're moving wires?" says Bert, stepping back, his fists unclenching, his voice softening. "I got a new drill for my birthday. One of the cordless ones. Maybe I should bring it over."

Something inexplicable happens when a man

picks up a tool to do home repairs. Some force, as yet undescribed by science, but nevertheless well known to women, is set loose. It's a force that lures men away from their families and the things they are supposed to be doing to the place where hammers are being swung.

Maybe the act of a hammer moving through the air sets off a cosmic thrumming only men can hear. Or maybe when a man picks up a screwdriver, he releases an odour only men with tools can smell—a musty, yeasty sort of smell, with a hint of leather and WD40. Men in their backyards raking leaves and men in their basements listening to ball games on portable radios are seized by this odour the way the urge to migrate seizes lesser species. Suddenly they're thinking, *I don't belong here any more. I belong in another place. I should be doing something else, and I should take my coping saw with me just in case.*

Men can sense when a wall is coming down, and they can't help the fact that they have to be there to watch it fall, or better yet, help push it over.

It has been argued that the fall of the Berlin Wall had nothing whatsoever to do with the collapse of communism: it was just a weekend project that got out of control—thousands of German guys satisfying their undeniable urge to fix things up.

Carl Lowbeer, himself of German descent, was the next neighbour to arrive at Dave's house on this Saturday morning.

He burst through the front door without knocking. Dave and Jim looked up to see him standing in the kitchen.

"Hi," said Carl, trying to slow himself down, trying to act nonchalant.

"Need any help?"

He was carrying a bright yellow thing about the size of an electric drill (except more dangerous-looking). It looked like a cross between an Uzi and a woodpecker. It was his reciprocal saw.

Carl got the saw last Christmas. It is his pride and joy. But there are only so many holes a man can cut in his own house before he is told to stop. The saw spent most of the summer on Carl's worktable in the base-ment—calling to him.

At the end of August, when Carl's wife, Gerta, went downstairs with a load of laundry and found him cutting random holes in a sheet of plywood, she took the saw away from him. She said he could have it back if he stood in front of the house on Saturday mornings with a sign around his neck that read *Need Holes Cut?*

By noon there were seven men in Dave's kitchen. Two of them friends of Jim Scoffield's whom Dave had never met—guys with tools.

Carl was in the living room, huddled on the sofa beside Bert Turlington. Bert was demonstrating his new electric drill. The drill had more gears than a Maserati. Bert was revving the motor and explaining what it could do. He handed the drill to Carl, who didn't expect it to be so light.

"Oops," said Carl, holding it too close to Morley's Brazilian hardwood coffee table. The drill skitted across the table leaving a long white streak in the dark finish, such as a skater might leave on a freshly flooded rink.

"That's okay—don't worry, don't worry," said Bert, spitting on the table and rubbing the gouge with the palm of his hand. "I have something at home that will cover that."

Things were lurching along at about the same pace in the kitchen. There were now a series of twelve melon-sized holes punched in the kitchen wall at two-foot intervals, leading from the light switch by the back door to the hole where Dave intended to install the plug for the toaster.

Twelve holes and seven busy men.

Jim and Dave were routering putty out of the broken window. Phil Harrison was sucking up plaster dust with Carl Lowbeer's Shop Vac. The two men Dave didn't know were racing a pair of belt sanders along a couple of two by fours they had set on the floor. Everyone was productively occupied—except for Carl Lowbeer, who was sitting at the kitchen table, morosely cradling his unused reciprocal saw and watching the belt sanders shudder along.

Counting Bert Turlington's electric drill, there were, at noon on that Saturday, six power tools operating in Dave's house.

And noon on Saturday was the moment when Sam arrived downstairs, rubbing his eyes, taking in the chaos of his kitchen and asking the most reasonable question.

"What's for breakfast?"

"Toast," said Dave. He said this without turning the router off or even turning around. Sam stared at his father's back for a moment, then shrugged and dropped a couple of slices of bread in the toaster. As soon as he pushed the handle down, the toaster began a loud and peculiar buzzing. No one could hear it over the din of the tools. Except Sam, who said, "What's that?"

No one heard Sam either.

Then the lights went out.

And the tools died.

In the sudden silence someone, perhaps Bert Turlington, said, "Do you smell that?"

It was an elusive odour, but it was there.

Somewhere.

"I think it's coming from behind this wall," said Jim Scoffield.

"*This* wall," said Carl Lowbeer.

Sam watched the men, some of them bent over at the waist, some standing on their toes, all of them sniffing the walls, the ceiling, the cupboards.

And then there was smoke hanging in the air like wisps of fog.

Someone said, "We overloaded the wires. The wires are burning—cut the wall open over here."

And Carl Lowbeer jumped up and said, "My saw works on batteries." And he lurched towards the wall, revving his reciprocal saw in front of him. Before anyone could stop him, Carl had cut a hole in the wall the size of a loaf of bread.

"Not there," said Bert Turlington. "Here."

"Coming. Coming," said Carl, moving around the kitchen like a mass murderer. He cut a second hole five feet down the wall.

Sam's eyes were as wide as saucers.

"I've got a fire extinguisher in the truck," said one of the men Dave didn't know.

They found the remnants of the fire with the third hole. A mouse nest leaning against the overheated wires. It had burned itself out. The man with the fire extinguisher gave it a blast.

"Just in case," he said.

At twelve-fifteen Dave took stock of what they had accomplished: the broken window, the chipped sink, fifteen holes, the sodden plaster where they had used the extinguisher.

Arnie Schellenberger looked at Dave and said, "Uh, Dave, when's Morley coming home?"

Dave said, "Not until tonight, not until ten, eleven."

Arnie said, "There's an electrician I know from the plant. He might come over. If you did the window he could do the wiring and we could patch the holes by—" he looked at his wrist "—ten?"

The electrician, Ted—black jeans, black jeans jacket, earring—arrived at five. He looked around the kitchen and pointed at the knob-and-tube wiring and crossed his arms.

"I can't repair that. It's the law. Whatever you've exposed I have to replace."

He looked at the expression of horror on Dave's face.

"You need this done tonight. Right?"

Dave nodded.

The electrician looked around, "You guys got a reciprocal saw?"

Carl Lowbeer's hand shot into the air like a school-child's. "I do. I do," he said way too fast and about an octave too high. Everyone turned and stared at him. Carl looked down and said it again, this time slower and a register lower. "I do," he said.

The electrician pointed at the back wall of Dave's kitchen. "We're going to pop out the drywall," he said. "Take the wall down to the studs. That way I can get at everything at once."

Dave was frowning.

"It's the fastest way," said the electrician.

He looked at Carl.

"Cut around the top by the ceiling and along the baseboard. We'll pop it out, nice and simple."

Carl was beaming.

He was about to sink the saw into the wall when the electrician held up his arm.

"You guys turned the electricity off. Right?"

Everybody stopped and looked at each other.

Morley came home soon after nine.

When she turned onto their street, she noticed her house looked strangely dark.

She pulled into the driveway and parked the car and gathered an armful of junk, her purse, a sweater, some files. She headed towards the back door. She was exhausted. She dropped a file and stooped to pick it up. It was only then that she noticed the warm glow of candles flickering through the back window. She felt a wave of affection wash over her.

Dave had made a romantic meal.

She had barely eaten all day. She was smiling as she opened the back door. She put her purse down and called, "Hello." She stopped dead in her tracks.

Sometimes you are confronted by things that are so far from what you expect that your brain is unable to process what it is looking at. There is a momentary disconnect between what you think you are looking at and what you are actually looking at. Morley looked around her kitchen. There were candles everywhere. And flashlights and snake lights. And men. There were four men in the kitchen. All of them on their hands and knees.

The four strangers on their hands and knees were staring at her the way a family of raccoons might stare at her from the back deck. She thought, *This is not my house. This is not my kitchen. This is a frat house. This is a fraternity party.*

As her eyes adjusted to the light, she took in more details. The men were holding tools. There was a pile of pizza boxes on the floor. And an empty case of beer. Sam, her son Sam, was sprawled beside the pizza boxes. Asleep. What was he doing in a frat house? This couldn't be her kitchen—two of the walls were missing. She looked at the men again.

One of them stood up.

"Hi. I'm Ted," he said, "the electrician. We'll have this cleared up in just a minute or two."

And then she saw Dave, her husband, crawling towards her. He stopped about ten feet away. "Hi," he said.

He waved his arm around the room—at the broken window, the holes in the wall, the back wall that had completely disappeared—and he said, "We're fixing the toaster."

This *was* her kitchen.

Morley's mouth opened, but no words came out. It closed, then it opened again. She *seemed* to be trying to say something. Dave nodded, trying to encourage her, as if they were playing charades. Her mouth kept opening and closing, opening and closing, but no sound came out.

Then without saying anything—not one word—Morley turned around and walked out of the house. She got in her car and backed out of the driveway.

Dave said, "She'll be back in a minute."

Bert said, "I think I should be going."

Carl said, "Me too."

Dave said, "Maybe if we could just get the power on before she comes back."

Morley wasn't back in a minute. She wasn't back for nearly an hour.

When she did return, she walked across the kitchen and opened the freezer door. About a cup of water trickled onto the floor. She let out a muffled sob.

Dave helped her empty the freezer. They deposited plastic bags of food in an assortment of neighbourhood fridges. "They're all within easy walking distance," Dave pointed out helpfully.

When they had finished unloading the fridge, Morley went into the living room and met Jim Scoffield's two friends. They were still sitting at her coffee table. They had a naphtha gas camping lantern resting on the arm of a chair and were playing cards in its garish light. When Morley came in the room, one of the men looked up and said, "Are there any subs left?"

The renovation took six weeks to finish.

Dave worked on it alone until the middle of the next week. He reconnected the electricity on Tuesday, but when Morley came home she got a shock when she tried to open the refrigerator, which, unfortunately, was the first thing she tried to do. So he shut the power off again and rechecked everything and turned it on the next morning. Everything seemed to be working fine until Sam came home from school and showed them how he could turn the microwave on with the TV remote.

There was a thunderstorm that night. Morley became increasingly agitated with each lightning flash. She had read stories about women washing dishes at the kitchen sink and WHAMMO! they get hit by lightning. Cows, golfers, people in boats—why not her kitchen? She didn't trust the wiring.

They called an electrician to finish the job: a methodical and trustworthy man. It was the electrician

who spotted the lead pipes running into the upstairs
bathroom, and he said, "If you want to have them
replaced you might as well do it while you have the
walls down."

So they had the plumbers in and had the entire
upstairs bathroom redone, and downstairs, where the
back wall was, Morley had one of those bay windows
put in, which is something she has always wanted. She
has a herb garden going in the window space.

It was six difficult weeks and they had to get a new
vacuum because the old one got clogged with plaster
dust, but the upstairs bathroom is lovely and so is the
bay window with the plants in it.

Dave was admiring the plants two weeks later,
standing in front of the window and looking out into
the yard, enjoying the new view. You can just see the
alley over the back fence. He was standing there
staring out the new window and into the alley when
Ted Bescher drove by in his TR6.

But it is a beautiful window . . . and Dave likes it,
especially in the evening when the light is soft. In the
morning too, especially Saturday mornings, when the
kids are still in bed. It's lovely to sit in the kitchen
together—the sun drifting down on the coriander,
Morley and Dave sipping coffee and reading the paper.
They were sitting there one Saturday morning in
October, two months after the renovation was finished,
when Morley stood up and walked over to the counter
to make some toast. She turned and smiled at Dave and

said, "Don't you think it would work better if we could plug it in at the table? So we wouldn't have to get up and walk across the kitchen every time someone wanted toast?"

The Razor's Edge

It was about ten years ago that Dave came home from a visit to Cape Breton with his uncle Jimmy's electric razor. He didn't steal the razor—his aunt Elisabeth, Jimmy's wife, Jimmy's *widow,* gave the razor to Dave. Elisabeth, who is eighty-seven years old, lives alone in Halifax, in a rambling wooden house on Chestnut Street, a stone's throw from the university.

Elisabeth, who Dave tries to visit every time he is in town, has been parcelling out Jimmy's possessions to relatives for twenty-five years. On previous trips and trips subsequent to the electric razor, Dave has walked out of Elisabeth's with a wooden-handled hairbrush, a wool jacket, a thick black-and-gold ballpoint pen and a stuffed duck.

"This used to be your uncle's duck," Elisabeth said, as she handed it to him.

Dave stood dumbly by her door, holding on to the duck, his suitcase at his feet. What else could he say except thank you? What else could he do except march up to airport security with a duck under his arm?

They X-rayed it.

"It seems to be dead," said the security guard as he handed it back.

So many years have passed since his uncle Jimmy's death that Dave has wondered if some of the stuff he has lugged away from Elisabeth's *wasn't* in fact his uncle's. After twenty-five years you had to wonder if Elisabeth might have acquired some of these things since his leaving—at church sales perhaps, or maybe at Frenchies. It was entirely possible these things she was handing out weren't Jimmy's things at all. But whether they were or whether they weren't, it didn't really matter. They were heirlooms just by virtue of the way they had arrived in his life, and Dave could hardly drop them in a garbage can at the airport. So each time Elisabeth handed him something, Dave thanked her earnestly and dutifully lugged it home. Which is why he has a stuffed duck on the shelf in his bedroom closet. That's where he put the hairbrush and the electric razor too—on the shelf in his closet, out of the main current, but not out of the river of his life.

Dave's father, Charlie, was from a family of five children. Elisabeth is the last one of them left. Visiting Elisabeth is one way Dave can still visit his father, one way he can still reach out to Charlie. Elisabeth's children, Dave's cousins, have been trying to get her out of her house and into a home for almost a decade, ever since she began boiling all the tap water before she'd use it. Elisabeth started this a year or so before her eightieth birthday. At first, she only boiled drinking water, but now she boils everything. She boils the water she is going to cook in before she boils it for cooking. She boils her bath water. She has two power bars in her bedroom and eight electric kettles in a row. It takes her an hour to fill a tub.

"It's poison," she says, "but you can boil the poison out if you're careful."

Aside from her thing with the water, Elisabeth seems eminently capable of caring for herself. And her dramatic good health has given Dave pause about her water boiling.

The razor spent five years squirrelled away at the top of Dave's bedroom closet in its zippered leather case. One Saturday afternoon Dave was looking for a sweater and found the razor instead. He took it over to the bed and unzipped the leather case, and he found himself staring at this . . . this beautiful thing. It didn't look at all like an electric razor. Not at all. It looked more like a piece of decoration pried from an Airstream trailer, or a part shaken off a milkshake maker. It was a black-and-silver, torpedo-shaped, art deco relic. It was sleek. It was . . . Uncle Jimmy's.

Dave plugged the razor in. To his great surprise, it worked. And in that instant, the vibrating piece of antique chrome became *his* razor. In that instant Dave knew that Uncle Jimmy's razor would imbue the morning ritual of shaving with a new pleasure—the pleasure of continuity. The pleasure of touching the past.

Things are seldom that simple.

The *first* morning, Sunday, was simple. But the second morning, right in the middle of the job, the razor's motor cut out, leaving Dave staring in the bathroom mirror with the razor clinging to his beard like a leech.

The last thing you want to do if an electric razor freezes on your beard is try to pull it off. There is no telling what might happen if you do. You have to be clever about these things.

Well, first you have to take a moment to panic.

You imagine yourself hunching into the nearest emergency room, the razor dangling from your face and some smart-alec intern grabbing it and grinning. You imagine him saying something like *This might hurt a bit.*

So you don't go to the hospital—you work at it yourself. After Dave had fiddled with the razor for a few minutes, he got it back to life by twisting the electric cord and holding the razor at a careful angle. Nothing to it. If he held the cord in the correct position the razor worked fine. So shaving became a two-handed job: one hand to hold the razor, the other to twist the cord. As long as he got the angle right, the razor behaved.

This worked fine for a couple of years, but all the twisting and turning eventually took its toll on the electric cord. The razor got crankier and crankier, and one morning Dave finally got fed up. *This is ridiculous,* he thought.

He headed off to the basement with Uncle Jimmy's razor. He was going to fix it.

There are many satisfactions in this beautiful life, but one of the great satisfactions, up there with great meals and great friendships, with love and afternoon naps, is fixing something that is broken.

The devil himself could slide down the basement stairs when a man is engrossed in fixing an electric razor, scratch a match on a wooden beam, smile and say, *Excuse me. I didn't mean to startle you, sir. But I thought you'd like to know that upstairs in your living room there is a woman waiting for you. And she knows all your secret desires and all your secret wishes. All of them, sir. You might say she is the woman of your dreams. If you would just put that screwdriver down and follow me up those stairs you could make her acquaintance. Sir? Surely you would like that. There could be no harm in that. Surely. I know you would like to meet her. For she is part Hayley Mills from the original* Parent Trap. *And she is part Audrey Hepburn from* Wait Until Dark. *And she is also part Lisa Bonet from that movie that was censored, and I don't think you have seen the uncut version of that film. Have you? Sir? The part with the chicken blood? Well that's the part that is playing upstairs. Right now. In your living room. Sir. And your family won't be home . . . for hours. That's all arranged. Sir.*

The devil could puff on his cigarette and say all that, and oh yes, some men would go. (Even some family men would go.) But not if they were fixing something. If they were fixing something *you* know what they would do—they would wave their screwdriver absentmindedly in the air and say, *I'll be up in a minute. I am just about done here.* But they *wouldn't* be up in a minute, because you are never *just about done* when you're fixing things.

Dave took the back off the electric razor. The simplicity of it was what startled him. All he found inside was a tiny motor and some vibrating teeth. He had expected . . . more. With the back off, it looked like a toy razor. There were some little blue-coated condensers and a few other wiry odds and ends, but that was about it.

Everything was so small, Dave wasn't sure how he was supposed to repair it. He found a loose connection and tried to glue it into place, but that proved unsatisfactory. He was worried about electrical arcing, so he covered the join with electrical tape. When he plugged the razor in and it didn't work at all, he thought, there's nothing to lose. So he got out his soldering gun and resoldered every connection he could see. Then he replaced the electric cord with one he removed from an old tube radio, and he soldered that. He covered all the joins with more electrical tape and by the time he had finished there was so much solder and so much electrical tape, he couldn't get the chrome cover back on. But the razor was working.

So he got a roll of duct tape and wound the whole thing around with duct tape, and he was back in business. It was a different kind of shave. Since he now had to be careful about electric shock, he could no longer grip the razor manfully. He had to hold it with his fingertips. It was by no means as elegant as it had once been—he wouldn't let anyone else in the bathroom when he was using it—but it was functional, and it was Uncle Jimmy's, and he had fixed it himself, and that gave him a certain pleasure.

He still had the chrome case. He intended to get it repaired one day. When he could find someone to repair it. When he had time to take it to them. In the meantime, he was worried about dirt fouling the circuitry, so instead of the leather case, he kept the razor in a Ziploc plastic sandwich bag.

He used it every morning and even took it with him when he went away. He had it in his suitcase when he rushed out the door at quarter past six one morning, horribly late for the seven o'clock plane that he was supposed to be taking to New York City. Danny Kortchmar's daughter was getting married at noon. The wedding was a three-hour drive from Kennedy Airport up the Hudson River. It would be close, but if he made it to the plane, he'd make it to the church. Danny used to play guitar with James Taylor, among others, and Dave and Danny went way back.

As Dave squealed out of his driveway, his bag bouncing on the seat beside him, a tie crammed in his pocket, he glanced at the clock on the dashboard and began to calculate exactly what he had to do to make his plane. It would be tight. But if everything went without a hitch he might make it. He *would* make it. He'd make it. He was going to make it.

It is always like this with Dave and airports—always. He is always late, egregiously late. He never arrives an hour before a flight. Half an hour is too early for Dave. Those are airport rules, and Dave doesn't play by airport rules. Airport rules are for everyone else. Dave thinks he is better than airports. He thinks he can cheat time; he thinks he can outplay time. He thinks he can get more out of time than time is going to give him. Airport time, anyway.

As a road manager Dave was responsible for moving bands and their equipment around the country, getting them from hotels to arenas and from dressing rooms to stages on time. This was something, it turned out, he was very good at. He was able to instil a sense of schedule into a collection of individuals whose body clocks often ran in time zones that have yet to be discovered. Now he manages to open his record store, the Vinyl Cafe, more or less on schedule every morning, compared to, say, Kenny Wong, whose cafe keeps more quixotic hours. But put an airplane ticket in Dave's hand and the equation alters.

Morley has more than once pointed out that his recurring inability to conform to airport expectations is classic passive-aggressive behaviour.

Dave dismisses this.

"You are so wrong," he scoffs. "You have to have something *against* someone to be passive-aggressive. I don't have *anything* against airports. What could I possibly have against airports? Why would I have a thing about airports? One airport, maybe. But all airports? That's completely nuts."

He got so agitated the last time she brought it up that she vowed not to mention it again.

But look at him. Six-fifteen a.m.—forty-five minutes before an *international* flight—leaning forward over the wheel, squinting at the cars ahead of him, weaving in and out of traffic. He never drives like this. Forty-five minutes to go, and he thinks he is okay. And what is he repeating over and over to himself?

I'm going to make it. I'm going to make it.

Maybe he will. He has done it before.

But this is a Monday morning, and Dave is not used to Monday-morning driving. Monday-morning driving is bleary-eyed, bad-tempered commuters struggling to hold on to the weekend. Monday-morning driving is coffee splashing out of coffee mugs, bran muffins crumbling onto laps. Monday-morning driving is lost sunglasses. And Monday-morning driving is . . . traffic jams.

Dave was a good five miles from the airport and doing fine when the traffic began to slow. A few minutes later he crested a hill and all he could see was brake lights forever—cars slowing and cars jerking to a stop and cars stretched out in front of him as if they were never going to move. Ever again.

Anyone else would have given up. But Dave was not about to give up. Not Airport Dave. Airport Dave didn't even think about quitting. He swung onto the shoulder and bounced five hundred yards along the gravel to the next exit. If the freeway was blocked, he would leave the freeway. He would bypass the traffic. He would go cross-country. He followed a semi-trailer off the highway and into a landscape of low-rise warehouses.

A hundred and fifty years ago, settlers heading west were completely enveloped by the tall grass prairie. Big bluestem grew so tall that men on horseback had to stand in their stirrups to see the horizon. More than once a careless traveller who swung out of his saddle never saw his horse again. Sometimes all you could see of the wagon ahead of you was a canvas cover bouncing through the purple gayfeather, like a sail on a distant sea. Like a prairie schooner.

The two-storey warehouses that surrounded Dave were just as confusing. He had no clear idea where he was heading as he roared through the acres of flat buildings. And when the streets became long arcing curves, he completely lost his bearings. He tried to use the sun to navigate. He craned his neck out the car window desperately searching for a descending plane to give him a clue.

When he screamed into the airport parking garage fifteen minutes later, he left a trail of blue smoke.

He had twelve minutes until his flight was scheduled to leave. He was still muttering *I'm going to make it* as he slammed the car door behind him.

He had to check in, clear customs, immigration and security. He had to make it to his gate. But if there were no more hitches, he believed he could do it.

He was running for the terminal now, his tie half out of his pocket, his suitcase bumping against his leg. He was going to carry it on with him.

Maybe he *was* going to make it.

But when he burst through the automatic doors, he found himself smack in the middle of the terminal. This was the international terminal. He didn't know it well. Which way should he go?

He looked around the cavernous glass-walled building in panic. Everyone but him seemed to know where they were heading. Everything seemed to be in motion. The conveyor belts of luggage, a family carrying something in a blue plastic kennel, businessmen with their swinging briefcases, a golf cart beeping its horn as it whipped by him.

This was a moment for regrouping. Dave should have stopped for a moment, even a brief moment. He should have stopped and looked at his ticket, should have checked one of the departure screens hanging from the ceiling. But the clock was ticking, and there was a hundred yards of open terminal stretching in front of him. Without stopping to think where he was going, Dave began to run. He was working on straight instinct. He could read the screens on his way by them. If he was going the wrong way, so be it. He didn't have time to stop and think. As long as he was moving, he still had a chance. He still had ten minutes. Over and over he was repeating his mantra: *I am going to make it. I am going to make it*.

With eight minutes to go he got in the wrong check-in line—the first-class line. He chose it because it was the shortest. When he got to the counter the woman almost waved him away. But she could see the panic in his eyes. She took the fax he had pushed under her nose and said, "Where is your ticket?"

Dave said, "This is an electronic ticket. It says I don't need a ticket."

The woman behind the counter said, "That's only if you're in an American airport. In Canada you need a ticket."

Dave was about to argue, but the woman had already begun to print him a ticket, and miracles of miracles, it was already stuttering out of her machine. He grabbed it and was running again, lurching towards the next stop—immigration. The officer waved him through with a nod and a smile, and he was home free. There were still five minutes to go and he was still moving, still running. His shirt was untucked and his heart was pounding. He was sticky with sweat. But he was going to make it.

And that's when he hit security.

It's always at the moment when you think victory is yours that things start going wrong. Dave cleared the metal detector, and was waiting for his suitcase to clear the X-ray machine. So was the security guard. A heavy-set, thin-lipped Mediterranean woman.

She looked at the X-ray screen suspiciously, then looked up at Dave and said, "Open your suitcase, please."

Dave fumbled with the lock, trying to open the bag as quickly as he could—slowing himself down with his hurry.

The lock clicked open on the third try, and Dave took a step back from the table, looking at his watch, looking down the corridor towards his gate, looking desperately at the guard as she reached into his suitcase and pulled out his little Ziploc plastic bag. She held his razor in the air, swinging the ball of duct tape and dangling wires in front of his face.

She said impassively, "What is *this,* sir?"

It was the last thing he was thinking of. Everything else seemed so much more important. To get so close and stumble on the last hurdle. To have to phone home and face Morley, *I missed the plane,* as if she hadn't warned him a hundred times. As if she hadn't warned him that very morning.

He tried to get calm. He breathed deeply. He noticed that everything around him had ground to a halt. The hustle and bustle of the security check had stopped. Everyone was staring at him. He was surrounded by businessmen in business suits: men with sleek leather carry-on bags, men with cellphones, men carrying *The Wall Street Journal,* men staring at his corduroy pants and his suede shoes and his untucked shirt tail. They wanted to know the answer to the question as much as the security guard: What was this mess of tape and wires hidden in his luggage?

Dave felt his heart sink. A man's razor, after all, is a reflection of his masculinity, a symbol of his manhood.

He was surrounded by stud horses, all of them pawing the ground as they waited on his explanation.

"It's my razor," he said pathetically. He thought he heard one of the men whinny. He was engulfed by a wave of self-loathing.

But he still had four minutes before his plane was scheduled to leave, and he was not about to give up. Not yet. He focused on the guard standing in front of him, still dangling the razor in front of his face. He began to explain about his uncle Jimmy. The businessmen began shaking their heads, began walking away. Even the security guard wasn't listening to him.

"You are going to have to turn it on for me, sir," she was saying. "You are going to have to shave for me."

She spoke maddeningly slowly. As if Dave was a young child.

Dave was no longer thinking about Morley or the businessmen or even the security guard. All he could think about was his game plan, and his game plan was about to blow up in his face.

It was fight or flight.

Dave looked at the security guard and blurted, "I don't have time to turn it on. I don't have time to shave. You keep the razor. I don't want the razor. It's yours." Then he grabbed his suitcase and ran.

He ran down the corridor with his half-opened suitcase jammed under his arm, his other fist clenched and pumping the air. He ran with his head snapping back and forth, checking the gate numbers as he flew along. He ran as fast as he could—thrusting the suitcase above his head as he squirmed through a confusion of conventioneers. He was propelled through the early-morning crowd by fear—not only the fear of missing his plane but another fear, a residue fear, a childhood fear—the fear of getting caught. He was sure he was being chased.

When he pulled up at his gate there were still forty-five seconds left before his flight was scheduled to leave, but there was no one around—no one. The gate was deserted. The sign behind the counter said New York, but there wasn't a soul in sight.

A departure gate has a certain funereal feel to it when it is devoid of passengers and animated clerks. Dave sensed there was something wrong. But he didn't stop moving. He couldn't stop moving.

For the forty-five minutes since Dave had left home he had been possessed of the determination of a migrating elk. All he knew, all he was conscious of, was the need to keep moving. He had been engulfed by that determination for so long that he wasn't about to drop it now, so he did something he knew he wasn't supposed to do. He burst through the crash doors and began to lurch along the corridor looking for the tunnel that would lead him to his flight. As the doors swung shut behind him, they made an ominous click. *Whoops,* thought Dave, *maybe I shouldn't have done that*. But there was nothing to do now but keep going. He followed the deserted corridor until he came up against another door. It was locked. And it wouldn't open. He stood there foolishly. He tried the handle again, shaking it the way you might shake a recalcitrant vending machine.

He was so close—but he had apparently come to the end of the line. His shoulders sagged. He dropped his suitcase. He stood there without moving. And then simply because he couldn't think of anything else to do, Dave pulled out his ticket and stared at it: Toronto to New York, Flight #542. Departure 9:05 a.m. Not 7:05 a.m., 9:05 a.m. He should have felt like a fool. He didn't. He felt happy. He punched the air with his free fist. He was going to make it.

And not only that.

He could go and get his razor back.

He followed the passage back to the crash doors before he realized he wasn't going anywhere. He was in a no-man's land. All around him were locked doors that he couldn't open. He peered through a small window that looked back into the terminal. He waved at people heading towards *their* gates. He jumped up and down—trying to get someone's attention. No one noticed him. He felt like a little boy who had lost his mother at the supermarket. He turned back towards the plane. The only way out was to walk down the long hallway, through customs and back to where he started.

The cavernous customs hall was deserted save for two uniformed officers sitting at a desk, drinking coffee from Styrofoam cups. When Dave walked in, they both stared at him with complete amazement. It was seven in the morning—there wasn't an international flight due to arrive for an hour.

"Where did *you* come from?" they asked simultaneously.

They were more understanding than Dave could ever have hoped them to be. They let him through with a minimum of fuss, apologizing when they made him fill out a customs form. Regulations, they explained. Dave declared a carton of cigarettes and a bottle of Scotch. They took his form and pointed him down another long corridor. Two minutes later he was vomited back into the terminal, right where he began. He marched back through the airport, bypassing the ticket counter, carefully avoiding the immigration clerk who had processed him not fifteen minutes earlier.

And back to security, standing patiently in line until he came face to face with the same guard.

"Aren't you the guy with the razor?" she said, reaching for her walkie-talkie.

"I changed my mind," said Dave. "I want it back."

Someone produced a long extension cord and she made him turn it on. She motioned at his face. He asked if they couldn't do that somewhere out of sight. There must be a little room? She didn't even acknowledge the request. He had to shave beside the X-ray machine. It felt as if he was taking down his pants in public. But he was beyond embarrassment.

She waved him on.

"Okay," she said.

He got a coffee and a doughnut and went right to his gate. There was still an hour and half before his flight. There was a clerk there now, but Dave was the first and only passenger.

He sat down and smiled at her. She smiled back.

"You're early this morning," she said.

He nodded calmly, serenely.

"I always try to be," he said. "I've never understood those people who wait until the last moment."

Morley's Christmas Pageant

The annual holiday concert at Sam's school is a December celebration with a thirty-seven-year tradition that has been struggling for an identity of late— ever since the school board decreed that any December pageant must acknowledge the cultural diversity of the school. It's a dictum that does not sit well with certain parents—and changes to the concert have been debated passionately over the past few years.

Efforts to find a middle ground, to accommodate both the Christmas traditionalists and the Board of Education have met with varying degrees of success. Last year's "Solstice Celebration" made no mention of Christmas until the end of the show, when the grade-three class lined up on stage holding big cardboard letters that spelled out Merry Christmas. One by one, kids stepped forward with their letters and shouted out their greeting:

M is for Muslim, E is for Ecumenical, R is for Reform Jew.

When they got through Merry and it was time for the C in Christmas, Naomi Cohen held up her big green C and sang out, C is for Chanukah; and then

Moira Fehling, who was standing beside her, held up her red H and said, H is for Hanukkah too.

Then the grade threes sang, "Dreidl Dreidl Dreidl."

That was Lorretta McKenna's grade three. Loretta was perky and keen and full of ideas like that. She didn't come back this year.

The concert managed to offend so many parents, on both sides of the issue, that a committee was struck to review the whole idea. It was Rita Sleymaker, the committee chair, who came to Morley in April and asked for her help.

"You're in theatre," she said. "We want to put on a musical. A holiday sort of musical. We were hoping you would direct it."

"I can't imagine anything I would rather do," said Morley. Although she had no trouble imagining other things she would rather do as soon as she had hung up.

"I would rather have a needle in my eye," she said to Dave that night. "But I couldn't say no."

Morley began attending the Wednesday-evening committee meetings. When she came home from these meetings, it would often take her hours to wind down.

"They're all crazy," she'd say, pacing back and forth. "I'd rather chew tinfoil than go back next week."

But before summer vacation her impatience began to dissipate.

"We're getting to the meat of it," she said one night in June. "It's down to *The Wizard of Oz* or *Frosty the Snowman.*"

Frosty won. It was the perfect play for the pageant. They could do it without carols or mention of Christian tradition.

"It captures the true spirit of the season," said the school trustee enthusiastically when the script was sent to her. "It has music. And shopping."

Morley spent the summer rewriting *Frosty the Snowman,* essentially expanding the play so there would be a part for all 248 children. She added lots of street scenes, and when she was finished, there was a role for everyone, including a cameo for the principal, Nancy Cassidy, whom Morley coaxed into playing a talking pine tree.

In September there was an unexpected registration bubble, and Morley found herself a dozen roles short. She fussed with the script for a week, until, in a flash of inspiration, she added a narrator. She conceived of the narrator as a chorus, a chorus that would easily soak up the twelve new kids and any others who wandered along before Christmas. All her early reluctance had given way to outright enthusiasm. She had her arms up to the elbows in the mud of this play.

"This is fun," she said to Dave one night as she collated scripts. She couldn't wait to get going, couldn't wait to start with the kids.

The Saturday before the auditions were scheduled, parents began showing up at the house offering help. Katherine Gilcoyne was first.

"I'm a seamstress," she said. "I'm sure there'll be lots of sewing. I'd love to help with the costumes."

Morley was delighted. They had coffee and talked about the play and then, after an hour, when she was leaving, as if it was just an afterthought, Katherine reached into her purse and pulled out a brown manila envelope.

"This is Willy's résumé," she said.

Willy was her son. Willy was in grade five.

It was a twenty-page résumé, including an eight-by-ten glossy.

"He really wants to be a snowman," said Katherine, standing in the doorway. "Get him to recite his Lions Club speech. He won the gold medal. I think he would make a great Frosty."

Ruth Kelman arrived about an hour later. Right-to-the-point Ruth. "I heard you weren't considering girls for the snowmen," she said, her arms folded across her chest. Her car was in the driveway, still running. Her daughter, Joanne, was sitting glumly in the passenger seat; her husband was in the back.

Seven-year-old Joanne has been the breadwinner in the Kelman family for three years: the star of a series of soap ads and an obnoxious peanut-butter commercial. Ruth spends her life jetting around town with her daughter, lining up at one audition after another.

"What's the difference," said Morley sourly when they were gone, "between those auditions and a rug factory. If they got Joanne a job in a rug factory, they wouldn't have to spend all those hours waiting around at auditions."

As the rainy mornings of November folded into dark December afternoons, the play gradually took shape. The children were slowly settling into their roles. There were, eventually, four Frostys—two girls and two boys. At the beginning of the month, however, with only three weeks to go before the big night, no one knew the lines by heart, not even Joanne Kelman, whom Morley had cast as a villainous troll. But everyone was coming along, and Morley trusted the kids would eventually arrive where they should. Or close enough. Besides, there was a bigger problem than unlearned lines.

The story, as Morley had rewritten it, turned on a flashback—a scene in which Frosty recalled his days as a country snowman. For the all-important farmyard scene Morley had drafted Arthur and cast him as a sheep. Arthur, a docile and well-behaved dog by nature, did not adjust easily to the stage. The first few times Morley Velcroed Arthur into his sheepskin, he stood in the wings and refused to move, staring balefully out from under his sheep ears in abject humiliation. But as the weeks progressed Arthur underwent a character change. He grinned whenever he saw his costume, curling his lips back so you could see his teeth, flattening his ears and squinting his eyes. It was while he was dressed as a sheep that Arthur sniffed out and ate the contents of every lunch bag from Miss Young's grade-four class. He had his sheep costume on when he devoured the huge gingerbread house that Sophia Delvecchio had constructed and donated to the school. And it was while he was dressed as a sheep that he snarled at Floyd, the janitor, when Floyd found him padding down the corridor heading for the cafeteria.

The closer they came to opening night, the more problems Morley uncovered. The afternoon they moved rehearsals into the auditorium, it became clear that there was not enough room for everyone on stage.

"The stage isn't big enough for the narrators," said Morley to Dave one afternoon on the phone after rehearsal.

It was Dave's idea to erect scaffolding and put the chorus of narrators on what amounted to a balcony.

"Perfect," said Morley. "Brilliant."

Dee Dee Allen's father, who was in construction, said he could provide scaffolding.

Morley had thought one of the benefits of working on the play would be an opportunity to get to know some of the kids. Mostly she got to know Mark Portnoy. Mark who couldn't sit still. Mark who spent one entire rehearsal pulling the window blinds up and down, up and down. Mark who tied Jane Capper's shoelaces together. Mark who brought a salamander from the science lab to technical rehearsal and dropped it into Adrian White's apple juice.

Late one afternoon when she thought she was the only person in the school, Morley came across Mark in the grade-five classroom. He was going through a desk with a suspicious intensity. She had a feeling it wasn't his desk.

"Hello, miss," he said guiltily when he saw her, picking up his bag and leaving the room.

Morley now had a constellation of mothers orbiting her. Alice Putnam, overweight and perpetually cheerful, was in charge of the refreshment committee. Pale, gaunt and efficient Grace Weed was in charge of programs. Patty Berg, loud but trustworthy, was in charge of decorations.

By the beginning of the second week of December, life at the school had built to a fever pitch—all pretence of academics had vanished. Everything was focused on Thursday night's performance. When the kid's weren't rehearsing, they were waiting to rehearse—or making decorations.

Patty Berg's decoration committee had transformed the school into a riot of red and green. There were streamers and balloons in the halls and large murals on scrolls of brown paper. Frank Quarrington of Quarrington's Pizza Palace had donated Santa Claus pictures for the grade twos to colour: Santas with their jackets off and their sleeves rolled up—rolling dough and flinging it in the air.

There were five Santa images in all—each one in the pizza motif. The grade twos fell on them with gusto—everyone except Norah Burton, who brought hers to the front in tears.

"I can't colour this," she said, holding out her paper. It was a picture of Santa Claus standing over a kitchen table, doling out pizza slices to a group of ravenous elves. "Those are anchovies," said Norah, pointing at the pizza. "I hate anchovies." And she broke into tears.

"Those aren't anchovies, sweetie," said Mrs. Moffat, putting her arm around the little girl. "Those are green peppers."

"What are these little hairy parts?" asked Norah sobbing. "They look like anchovy legs. Green peppers don't have legs."

"That's just mould," said Mrs. Moffat sweetly. "The green peppers have gone off."

"Oh," said Norah.

On Wednesday the kids were sent home early with instructions to return at six o'clock with their costumes and props. They were to assemble in the science lab, where they would be supervised by a group of parent volunteers. The parents would use walkie-talkies to maintain contact with the auditorium. They would send the kids to the stage as they were needed.

The kids were told they could bring quiet games to play while they waited for their cues: cards, books, stickers—no Walkmans, no video games.

At five-thirty Morley phoned Dave in a panic. Floyd, the janitor, couldn't get the P.A. working.

"No one will hear the narrators," said Morley. "Help!"

As a young man Dave had spent fifteen years on the road with so many rock-and-roll tours he had forgotten half the places he had been to. If anyone could rustle up a working sound system in a hurry, it was Dave.

"No problem," he said. "I'll look after it."

"I love you," said Morley. And hung up.

The doors to the auditorium were scheduled to open at seven. By six-thirty the room was already half full and beginning to heat up. Half an hour later families were still streaming in.

There is something about sitting on a plastic chair several sizes too small for you that puts you in touch with feelings you never knew you had, especially if you have come to this chair on a cold December night, in a bulky winter coat, and there is no place for you to put the coat, except in your lap. Especially if the room is hot, and getting hotter, and there are little children everywhere, children in constant motion, like fields of seaweed waving on the ocean floor—small sticky children wiggling by you with cupcakes and glasses of lemonade.

You sit in your tiny seat with your coat in your lap, and you have thoughts that you will never share with anyone. Not even your therapist. Because the things you are thinking are so depraved you *couldn't* share them with anyone. Especially your therapist.

On Thursday night, at a quarter to seven, Pete Eckersall was sitting on one of the chairs at the back of the hall thinking awful thoughts. Pete hadn't eaten all day—and he was beginning to feel dizzy. Sitting in his tiny seat, his knees up near his shoulders, his parka open, his tie undone, his fedora pushed back on his head, he stared dolefully at the Rice Krispie square he had bought for dinner. It was Pete Eckersall's sixteenth straight Christmas pageant. He has a daughter in university, a son in grade five and most depressingly a third child, another daughter, who is three. Pete was sitting in his chair doing the addition in his mind. There would be twelve more nights like this one in his life, he thought glumly as he watched the excited young fathers at the front of the room with their video cameras and their babies on their shoulders.

With twenty minutes to go Pete looked up and saw one of his three ex-wives walking down the far aisle— a long green fuzzy decoration that had snagged onto her sweater dragging behind her. He looked away.

At a quarter past eight, fifteen minutes after the concert should have begun, Dave still hadn't arrived with the sound system. Morley decided to start without him. As long as he got there before the narrators climbed onto the scaffolding at the beginning of act two everything would be fine.

On Morley's command the auditorium lights dimmed and the curtain rose. There was a pine tree standing alone at the centre of the empty stage. A murmur, which began in the front row, swept through the room when the pine tree took two steps forward and, row by row, people recognized the tree as none other than the school's principal, Nancy Cassidy. She was smiling gamely from the hole cut halfway up the costume—a costume Morley had spent two weeks convincing Nancy to wear. The murmur changed to applause and the applause grew—parents were whistling and stomping their feet. Nancy bowed awkwardly.

"Welcome," she said, "to our annual pageant."

Then she gasped as a papier-mâché moon dropped abruptly from the sky and swung across the stage in front of her face like a scythe.

"Sorry," said a tiny voice from the wings as the moon was pulled jerkily out of sight.

The grade ones opened the show. Parents craned their necks as the kids marched earnestly down the aisles, swinging their arms and singing. When they arrived on the stage, everything ground to a halt momentarily when Eli Rasminsky, who had the opening lines, stood on the stage staring at his shoes, frozen, until the gym teacher swooped out of the wings, held him up and spoke his lines for him.

All things considered, the rest of the act went smoothly. There were the awkward, but not unex-pected, missed cues: the children who waved inces-santly at the audience; the parents who sneaked out as soon as their child had performed; the parents holding crying babies who *wouldn't* leave; a Christmas tree that fell; but from her vantage point backstage, Morley was feeling, if not victorious, at least grateful when they arrived at the end of act one without a major disaster.

As the intermission began someone passed her a message from Dave. He was on his way with the sound system. As she faced the beginning of act two, Morley was feeling pretty good about things.

The kindergartners, who everyone thought were too young to include in the play, were set up to open the second half with a single song. They weaved onto the stage like a line of shift workers, peering out at the audience, waving and ponderously arranging themselves by height on the two benches set up on stage left. Bill Moss and Alan Schmeid changed places three times, finally standing back to back while Shirley Gallop measured them.

They were all carrying lit candles in little tin candle holders. They were going to sing "This Little Light of Mine."

As soon as they finally organized themselves into rows, you could see that Gretchen Schuyler was going to cry. Gretchen's candle had gone out. Her head was hanging down. And sure enough, as soon as the piano began and everyone started to sing, Gretchen's shoulders started to shake.

When no one came to her rescue, Gretchen really let loose: her hands covered her eyes, her shoulders shuddered, her sobs audible even over the singing. One by one everyone who knew them turned and stared at Gretchen's parents, who were pinned in the middle of the auditorium with smiles frozen on their faces—nodding at everyone as if nothing was wrong—unable to get to their daughter.

It was while everyone's eyes were on Gretchen that the stage door opened and a blast of cold air blew across the stage. As the cold air hit them, the kindergarten kids stopped singing and turned to stare at the apparition outlined in the door. It was a huge man with a ponytail, wearing motorcycle boots and a black T-shirt with the sleeves cut out. He was six feet four if he was a foot. He had a studded belt and ham-hock arms, a tattoo of a large bird on his shoulder and a scruffy beard. He looked like a biker.

Gretchen Schuyler was the last to spot him. Because he was the first adult within reach since her candle had gone out, Gretchen did the only thing she could think of doing. She ran across the stage and wrapped her arms around his legs.

Miss Perriton, the kindergarten teacher, climbed onto the stage. The biker grinned at Miss Perriton, and the kids could see he was missing teeth. Then he limped across the stage with Gretchen clinging to his leg like a brace and said, "Where do you want the speakers?"

Two other guys appeared through the door behind him, one unrolling a thick black coaxial cable, the other lugging a speaker the size of a Volkswagen. Dave was the last through the door. He was carrying a large control board.

"What are you *doing*?" said Morley when she pushed her way through the kindergartners and up to her husband.

"The best I can," said Dave.

They were not doing much better in the science lab (or "the holding tank" as Morley had begun to call it). There were too many kids crammed into too small a place for even the best of circumstances. And this was not the best of circumstances. The kids were so revved up that the walls seemed to be vibrating—the energy fuelled by a deadly combination of butterflies and boredom, nervousness and nerve. The parent volunteers who had been placed in charge had no experience with this many children in one place at one time. They didn't understand that if they didn't nip the first eruption in the bud, the room could go completely berserk.

And they were, unfortunately, too busy trying to figure out how to work their walkie-talkies to recognize just how dangerously close to that first eruption they were moving. The walkie-talkies hadn't been functioning well all night. They could hear Morley talking to them, but they couldn't make out what she was trying to say.

"It sounded," said Alice Putnam, frowning at her handset, "like she wanted us to send her a Hawaiian pizza."

The kids sensed their distraction. In one corner a group of grade sixes were circled around the infamous Mark Portnoy, watching with academic interest as he tried to feed his Ritalin to a boy in grade four. On the other side of the room three younger boys were trying to stuff Simone Newbridge into a supply cupboard.

Alice Putnam put down her walkie-talkie and looked around the science lab. The level of noise in the room was accelerating. She suspected that there were things happening she would be better off not knowing. Through the din, she thought she heard a muffled cry for help. It sounded as if it was coming from inside a cupboard. There was a fight on the far side of the room.

Alice couldn't decide if she should go for the fight or the cupboard. The room needed an iron hand and she didn't have one.

Which is when the door opened and Morley hit them with a blast of sound that shut everyone up.

"Street scene," said Morley. "We need the grade threes. We're starting."

Five minutes later everyone was on stage. Morley was standing at the back of the auditorium holding Dave's hand. They were waiting for the narrators to scramble up the scaffolding. Someone had lifted Gretchen Schuyler up with them. She was sitting on the edge of the platform, her feet swinging back and forth, clutching the candle that someone had finally lit.

Morley smiled at Dave as Mike Carroll stepped up to the microphone. Dave winked and reached down and flicked on the sound system. A small red light glowed on the board in front of him. He turned and smiled at Morley, who was holding her hands together, almost in prayer, leaning towards the stage. Mike— who was about to say his opening lines—paused and looked around. There was a hum in the room, an electronic hum that had begun when Dave turned the speakers on. A hum that had begun like the hum of a distant train but was growing louder and louder. People were looking around now, and no one could tell where it was coming from because it sounded as though it was coming from everywhere. Like the hum of creation, like the hum at the end of the world, like the hum of God himself.

The kids in the audience stopped moving, and babies in the front rows stopped crying, because it was a hum you felt now as much as you heard, and it felt as if the hum was going to swallow the room. Not knowing what to do, Mike Carroll leaned into the microphone and spoke his first line into the hum. He said, "Winter loomed."

Except he didn't sound at all like Mike Carroll in grade six saying "Winter loomed." Instead it sounded like the voice of God himself, and the words "Winter loomed" sounded more like "YOU ARE DOOMED."

Mike jumped back from the microphone, surprised at the sound of himself. Then there was a smell of smoke. Then a loud bang and then another one from each of the large speakers on either side of the stage. And then sparks. Not roman candles, more like cone-shaped eruptions of sparks. There were shrieks from the kindergarten kids, who had moved into the front row and were sitting on the floor in front of the speakers, and wild applause from the boys in grade six, and then the auditorium was plunged into darkness, and there was a moment of pure dark silence.

No one said anything. No one moved. Because no one dared move. It was so dark you couldn't see your hand if you held it in front of your eyes. There was darkness and a profound silence, until a small voice that sounded as if it might be coming from the stage called out one word: "MOMMY?"

And every mother in the hall answered as one. "YES!" they cried.

A chorus of mothers began to move tentatively towards the front of the hall. And then, the small voice called again out of the darkness, more urgently this time, "MOMMY." Mothers began to call their children's names out loud: "Gretchen," "Rodney," "Stacey," "Mark," "Billy," "I'm right here, darling," "I'm coming," "Stay where you are."

Mothers and fathers were moving instinctively towards the stage in the darkness—no one running, but moving as fast as they could—brushing the darkness in front of them with their arms, bumping chairs, knocking over glasses of lemonade, crushing Rice Krispie squares. Moving towards the voice in the darkness as their children began moving towards them. Then there was a soft whoosh and thump, and then another and another, as kids reached the edge of the stage and stepped off into the darkness. Children falling from the stage like lemmings in a Walt Disney nature movie. Mothers, carried forward on a wave of maternal anxiety, continued to push towards them. "Excuse me." "Excuse me," until suddenly the lights flared on again.

There was a moment of stock-taking, as they all tried to get their bearings.

There were no children left on stage. All the children had moved out into the auditorium and were standing and staring at the stage where they had been moments ago, staring at the seven mothers and one father who had actually climbed up there in the darkness. The parents squinting in the sudden light.

Morley hadn't moved. She was still standing beside Dave. Still leaning forward. Her hands still clasped as if in prayer. Dave was standing beside her. His hands still on his control panel . . . a look of horror on his face.

Dave was staring at Gretchen Schuyler, who was at the top of the scaffold, holding her lit candle over her head, as if it were an Olympic torch. The flame was only inches from the brass nozzle of the school's sprinkler system.

Out of the corner of his eye Dave caught Floyd, the janitor, moving towards Gretchen. Floyd seemed to be moving in slow motion, his arms stretched out. His mouth was opening and closing but no sound came out. He almost made it. But before he reached the scaffold, the heat from Gretchen's candle melted the safety nozzle and the water pressure in the sprinkler system blew. The fire alarm began to ring, and in the wink of an eye everyone was drenched, hair plastered down by the force of the water, as nozzle after nozzle popped open. They were ducking down, their hands over their heads as they fought their way out of the auditorium doors. It was like a British soccer riot.

Nancy Cassidy, who had changed back into her pine-tree costume for the closing number, was knocked over in the rush for the doors. When the school emptied, she was left in a stairwell spinning on her back like a beetle, unable to get herself up. When the firemen found her, Arthur was standing over her in his sheep costume licking her face. The firemen helped her up and out of her costume. Her carefully curled hair was hanging limply over her forehead; mascara streaked her cheeks.

"That dog was trying to kill me" was all she would say.

There were only two people left in the auditorium: Dave and Pete Eckersall—the survivor of sixteen Christmas pageants. Pete, who was still sitting in his chair when the firemen turned the sprinklers off, stood up and looked around, nodded at Dave and said, "Nice concert. I think I'll be heading home now." He walked out into the winter night, his soaked hair freezing in place as soon as he stepped outside.

When Dave got home, Morley was nowhere to be seen.

"She went for a walk," said Stephanie.

School was closed on Thursday and then unexpectedly on Friday too.

Morley was too mortified to go anywhere near anyone for the rest of the week.

On Friday night, however, she went to the mall with Sam, and they ran into the troublesome Mark Portnoy. He was kneeling in front of a pop machine by the supermarket doors—his arm stuffed into the machine all the way up to his elbow.

Morley watched him pull out a can of Dr. Pepper before he spotted her.

"Hello, miss," he said earnestly, slipping the pop smoothly out of sight. "That was an awesome concert. I'll never forget it."

He seemed to mean it.

Morley smiled and turned to go, but Mark wasn't finished with her. He followed her a few steps.

"Are you going to do it again next year, miss?"

Morley smiled. "I don't know," she said.

"I was wondering," he said, "if you do, I was wondering if I could run the sprinklers."

SOMEONE TO
WATCH OVER ME

Figs

On a rainy night in April, Dave sat down to write a letter he knew was going to be difficult.

Dear Tony, he began—that part was easy enough. *Dear Tony,* he wrote, his heart sinking as he stared at the expanse of white left on the page. Now what do you say?

You say it straight, that's what you do.

He began again. *Dear Tony, I am worried about your father.* Dave stared at those six words. He crumpled the page, threw it in the air, caught it, and without turning to look, he drifted it over his shoulder towards a wicker wastepaper basket on the far side of the room. He turned to see how he had done. Not even close. He sighed, stood up and retrieved the paper, came back to his chair and started again on a fresh page.

Dear Tony,
    It is still chilly here in the mornings, but by noon, most days, spring seems to be poking gamely about. We had a female warbler at the feeder last weekend, and a cardinal has been hanging around your father's backyard for weeks.

He stopped and stared at the ceiling. *This is ridicu-lous,* he thought. *Who cares about the weather? What do birds have to do with anything?* He crumpled *that* page up and threw it at the wastepaper basket, looking this time, missing again. He slipped his favourite Stan Getz album on the record player, but as soon as the warm sax filled the room Dave stood up and began pacing. He walked into the kitchen and stared out the kitchen window. It was quarter to nine. It was already as dark as the night would get. He poured himself a drink. He sat down at the kitchen table. He was there fifteen minutes later, staring at the kitchen clock as the second hand swept around to the hour, counting it down under his breath—five, four, three, two . . . one.

When 8:59 became exactly nine o'clock he turned and gestured grandly towards the window, towards his neighbour's house, waving his arms like a magician who was about to produce a cage of doves out of thin air, waving like an orchestra conductor who wanted his orchestra to begin. When nothing happened, Dave waved a third time, impatiently. This time, as if on his cue, his neighbour's lights snapped off, plunging their house into abrupt darkness. A thin smile settled on Dave's face.

"*Voilà,*" he muttered.

Dear Tony . . . He was writing the letter in his head now.

Dear Tony, I am worried about your mother and father.

Dear Tony, I thought I should write to you about your parents.

Dear Tony, Morley and I are concerned about Eugene and Maria.

Sheesh.

Dear Tony, Last fall, after Eugene's birthday party, you asked me . . . no . . . you asked us . . .

Dear Tony, Last fall after Eugene's birthday party you came to our house and asked us if we would keep an eye on your parents. It has been a long winter . . .

Dave ran his hand through his hair and stood up. This was like treason. He poured himself another drink. It was none of his business. No, it was his business.

Tony lives in London, England—he is in insurance. With Lloyd's. Tony's parents, Eugene and Maria, are Dave and Morley's next-door neighbours.

Tony had left home and moved to London well before Dave and Morley moved into the neighbourhood. Until Tony's anxious autumn visit, sitting right there, right in their kitchen, no, standing over there, by the kitchen door, getting right to the point—*I am worried about my parents*—Dave had seldom seen Tony. They had shaken hands over the backyard fence. They had talked briefly in the driveway and once on the sidewalk.

But for all that, Dave felt he knew Tony—because Dave has lived beside Eugene and Maria for almost twenty years. And when you are good neighbours, you know all about each other's family, regardless of where everyone lives. And Eugene and Maria are good neighbours.

Eugene, the eighty-nine-year-old vegetable gardener. Maria, the ninety-two-year-old cook. Maria, whose happiness when she is cooking for people is only surpassed by the happiness she feels when she's feeding them. It's a feeling of contentment that settles upon her like God's mercy, a feeling that arrives whenever there are hungry people sitting at her table, whenever she is carrying plates and platters back and forth across her kitchen.

Maria, who is living proof of the benefits of the Mediterranean diet, loves, more than anything, to prepare big lunches of sharp cheeses and fresh bread, sliced tomatoes and potatoes, onions and red bell peppers sautéed in olive oil and garlic. And chocolate. Squares of dark chocolate wrapped in white paper.

Maria, who loves to cook, was born with a twisted right leg. When she walks, her right knee brushes her left knee—her legs briefly forming the letter K with every step, her body pitching from left to right as if she were on the deck of a ship. Maria.

And Eugene, her husband, Eugene. The gardener. There isn't a square of sod left in Maria and Eugene's backyard. The whole yard has been turned for Eugene's vegetables. This is where Maria gets everything she cooks. Fat red tomatoes and large yellow potatoes. Sweet and hot peppers in every colour you could imagine: yellows, reds and greens. Long skinny beans. Rough chard and rapini. Sweet basil and pungent rosemary; mint and dandelions for salads; and vines of soft, juicy grapes.

Eugene harvests the grapes in late September, his hands purple and sticky. They are his secret ingredient. He mixes them lovingly with the boxes of grapes he buys from California and uses for the wine he and Maria barrel and store in juice bottles and pop bottles and old vodka bottles and any bottles they can get their hands on. Every autumn Eugene makes a red wine with a mysterious bouquet of a distant field of violets. He ages it in his collection of mismatched bottles in a cellar he dug under the back stairs thirty-seven years ago.

His grapevines—there are three—twist out of the ground by the garage. They come out of the ground as thick as Eugene's calf and wind down the back fence and over a grape arbour. This is where Eugene sits during the long summer afternoons when the sun is high and his back hurts from weeding. This is where he sits when all he has to do in the world is wait for his vegetables, tilting back on an old kitchen chair, watching the wasps dive-bomb the grapes that he breaks open and rests on his knees, smoking his *Parodis*—small, dark-leafed Tuscano-styled cigars that are no bigger than a pencil stub, but can last him over an hour. The cigars come in a red, green and white box—all the way from Italy. Eugene's dentist brings him a case every fall, in return for a trunkful of Eugene's home-made wine, which he drives home and carefully rebottles, corks and pastes with labels he has printed at a wine store. The

dentist, who undercharges Eugene for all his dental
work, has served the wine with great success at dinner
parties—always describing it offhandedly, whenever he
has been asked, as a private Italian bottling he has had
luck with. He has only confessed its true source once—
to a retired surgeon who knows about wine and keeps a
cellar in France, and who wasn't satisfied with the
dentist's vague explanation. He kept phoning and
phoning until he finally wore him down.

Now every fall the surgeon drives to Buffalo to visit
a tobacconist by the art museum who carries *Parodis,*
which he buys by the case, and smuggles into Canada
under the spare tire, and presents to Eugene proudly, in
return for *his* trunk of wine, which *he* only serves to
his family and best friends.

But it is not the grapevines that hold the place of
honour in Eugene's garden. Halfway down the yard,
halfway between the garage and the back door, within
easy spitting distance of his chair under the grape
arbour, is Eugene's pride and joy: his fig tree.

His fig tree is easily twenty feet high and produces
real figs, right in the middle of the city—figs that are
soft, green, pulpy and sweet. In late August and any
day in September, Dave can look out his window and
see Eugene—with his white moustache, and his white
shirt rolled to the elbows, and his dark blue vest, and
his old suit pants, and his small cigar—standing on a
ladder, picking fresh figs. He leaves the ones on the
lower branches for Maria, who can't climb the ladder
any more. Or for children who come into the yard.

"Mangia. Mangia," he says. "Good. It's good."

There is nothing, nothing in the world, that makes Eugene happier than the opportunity to invite a visitor into his yard to pick a fig and eat it while it is still warm from the sun.

Sometimes Dave has stood across the fence with the buzz of the summer cicada filling his head, and he has stopped what he was doing to watch Eugene on his ladder. Watching him, he has thought that the garden and the man were one—a piece of landscape torn out of the Italian countryside and dropped beside his yard, as if by magic. Looking over the fence, Dave has thought that the view from his backyard was as good as the view from any Umbrian hillside, that watching Eugene was as good as sitting on a hillside in Umbria with a headful of wine and a piece of soft cheese wrapped in brown paper for a companion.

Eugene's fig tree is the best-known tree in the neighbourhood.

Everyone knows about his tree because at one time or another everyone has bitten into one of his warm figs while Eugene stood beside them, watching carefully, smiling proudly.

Everyone knows Eugene grew the tree from a cutting he brought from his father's farm in Calabria, wrapped in a piece of linen, hidden in the bottom of his trunk.

Everyone knows that every October—before the first frost—Eugene digs a trench in his backyard, three

feet deep and three feet wide and thirty feet long. When
he has finished digging the hole, he carefully bends the
branches of the tree close to the trunk and ties them in
place. Then he digs around the roots until they are loose
and free of the earth, pushes the tree over and lowers it
into the trench with ropes. The leafless, bound tree looks
like a skeleton lying in the hole—the root ball looks like
a giant head, Eugene like a grieving relative as he covers
it, first with planks and then with earth.

He buries the tree.

If he left it standing it wouldn't survive the frost.
When Eugene has finished, except for the disturbed
earth, you wouldn't know anything was there. That is
where his fig tree spends the winter—bound and
buried, underground and out of sight, until the warm
April afternoon Eugene digs it out, and stands it up,
and cuts the branches loose.

The burial and resurrection of Eugene's tree have
marked the seasons in Dave's neighbourhood for
nearly fifty years.

Eugene and Maria came to Canada, from Italy, after
the war.

Eugene arrived via America. Via New York City.
He landed on New Year's Day in 1948. One of nine
brothers, he came to find a life.

He sent for Maria a year later. She landed at Pier 21,
in Halifax, on Christmas Eve, 1949. She left the beautiful Calabrian countryside in tears and was sick all
.the way over. When she landed, in the middle of a grey

Halifax afternoon, she vomited over the railing of the
S.S. *Mauritania* one final time.

Halifax harbour didn't even look real. It looked like
a black-and-white photograph of a harbour. How could
Eugene bring her to a country without colours? She
was crying when she phoned him. *What have you done
to me?* she asked.

Eugene landed a job in a restaurant as soon as he got
to Canada. By the time Maria arrived, he had a job in
a mattress factory. He worked on a machine that
shaped the springs. He worked eleven, twelve hours a
day. It was hard work, but he stayed at it for ten years.
Then he went to Rothmans, packing cigarettes. That
was his best job.

Soon they were able to buy a house. For the first five
years they lived in an apartment in the basement and
rented out the top two floors. They saved money.
Slowly they moved upstairs. One floor at a time.

Eugene worked hard. But he lived for the garden he
was building in the backyard.

He had grown up outside, barefoot, close to the land.
His family made their living growing figs. But as well
as fig trees he had grown up with grapevines and
orange trees and peach trees, with lambs and pigs, and
a cow and chickens. They had sheep as well. And a
donkey. When he was ten it was his chore to fetch
water. His father would strap wooden barrels onto the
donkey, and Eugene would ride it through the village
and fill the barrels at the well and walk it home.

Every night before bed Eugene's mother led them in an hour of prayer. His father would sit by the table with a rosary in his hand and hit anyone who fell asleep. In winter they would lie four kids to one bed, using coals from the fire in a steel bed-warmer. In the summer they slept outside on a platform in a large oak tree. They covered the platform with straw and then covered the straw with blankets.

They played hoops and soccer with a ball Eugene's older brother sent from the States. They threw stones against the school wall and bet who could get their rock closest. They used buttons for money. Eugene was in grade three the first time he bet. He came home holding up his pants, his shirt flapping open, every last button cut off his clothes.

When his grandfather died, he left Eugene his rifle. An antique two-chamber carbine. Eugene used it to hunt rabbits. When the war came, Eugene wrapped the rifle in linen and buried it in the yard. When the Germans left, he dug it up. The week before he left for America, he broke the rifle into two pieces and threw one half in the Adriatic and one half in the Mediterranean. He wanted to take the rifle with him to America, but he didn't want problems with immigration.

It all seemed like yesterday, but he had left home fifty-two years ago.

Dave and Morley bought the house beside Eugene and Maria two years before Stephanie was born. They moved in over a weekend in April and lived there for two months before Maria and Eugene acknowledged their presence.

It happened almost by accident. Morley was unloading groceries and she came face to face with Maria at the side of the house.

"We're your new neighbours," said Morley, resting her armload of food on the hood of the car, self-consciously holding out her hand. "My name is Morley."

Maria was carrying a basket of garden clippings towards the street. She nodded shyly, but she didn't put her basket down.

"Big house for two people," she said, leaving Morley by her car, her hand sticking out stupidly.

It took a year for the ice to thaw. Like any thaw it happened so slowly, so imperceptibly, that Morley didn't notice the change in the weather until it was over. It began with the washing. There is a solidarity that cannot be ignored between two women who still hang clothes outside to dry in the sun. It began one morning with a cautious smile when Maria and Morley found themselves, almost side by side, hanging sheets on their clotheslines. Then one day, to her surprise, Morley realized that she and Maria had started talking. It wasn't long before she realized that the only thing they were talking about was her pregnancy.

Maria, it turned out, was a veritable wellspring of reproductive advice. She was as ready as Morley's mother to unburden herself.

The morning Morley ran to throw up, Maria nodded happily. "Means baby will have lots of hair."

"Drink one coffee black every day," she told her one afternoon. "Baby will be quiet."

And when Morley started craving anchovies, Maria was delighted. "Smart baby. You will have a smart baby."

By the sixth month Maria had decided Morley was having a boy. She would point at her belly and smile.

"This is boy baby. A boy, this is." She would not explain how she could know the sex of the unborn child. "I know," she said, laughing.

Morley, who didn't like the superstition, and was growing impatient with the constant attention, tried to ignore her. But it rattled her. She didn't want to know the sex of her first child. And it worried her that Maria might know something. Her accent and old-world ways gave her credibility.

"Do you think she knows?" Morley would ask Dave. "Really? Do you think she does? How could she know?"

It was Dave who put his finger on it.

"Maybe," he said one night, "maybe she is telling you what she thinks you want to hear. Maybe she thinks she's giving you good news."

It had the ring of truth. And even though it made her sad to think that there were still people who thought having a son was better than having a daughter, it softened Morley, and it somehow excused Maria's intrusiveness. She was trying to be kind. She was operating out of good intentions. Morley wondered why Maria, who seemed so passionately interested in pregnancies and babies, had only one child.

Dave, meanwhile, was feeling profoundly uncomfortable every time he went into his backyard to relax. Every time he sat down with a beer, or the paper, or tried to listen to a ball game, there was Eugene on the other side of the fence, working on something. Dave couldn't imagine himself with a vegetable garden. Still, Eugene's activity made him feel inadequate. He took to turning his chair so that his back faced Eugene's yard.

Stephanie was born in September. Eighteen hours of labour. Seven and a half pounds. A week after Morley came home from the hospital Maria arrived at the front door for the first time ever. When Morley answered the bell, she was standing on the stoop, holding a basket of fresh tomatoes and a small wrapped present.

"For baby," she said, holding out the present. It was a hand-knitted sweater.

Morley felt awful. She was dishevelled and exhausted. She was wearing stained sweat-clothes. She was holding Stephanie (who had just spat up on her back) against her shoulder. She knew she should invite Maria in, but the house was as big a mess as she was. She couldn't.

A few days later Maria arrived again. This time with an armful of zucchini. As they stood awkwardly at the door, Maria spotted the basket of tomatoes still sitting on the floor where Morley had put them down. There was a cloud of fruit flies dancing around them like dust motes in the sun. They both stared at the basket. Without a word, Maria brushed past Morley, picked it up and left. Morley was horrified. She called Dave in tears.

That night, around suppertime, the doorbell rang again. It was Maria, this time with Eugene. She had turned the tomatoes into a rich pasta sauce. She was carrying a pot of penne with Italian sausage. Eugene was holding a dish of zucchini and rapini sautéed in garlic and olive oil. He had a loaf of fresh bread tucked under his arm and a bottle of wine sticking out of his pocket. They set everything on the kitchen table.

"Mangia. Mangia," said Eugene, backing awkwardly towards the door.

"We walk with baby," said Maria picking Stephanie up and carrying her to the stroller.

They were gone in under five minutes. They had spoken less than a dozen words.

They brought Stephanie back two hours later. She began to cry when they left.

And so they became neighbours. And slowly they found their way together. As the years passed it was clear that Eugene and Maria liked Morley and Dave and loved their kids. Maria continued to offer advice about child-rearing. She understood the pressures of early parenthood. She often arrived at the front door unannounced and took both kids for long walks— wandering patiently through the neighbourhood while Sam studied hubcaps and Stephanie poked at flowers.

These seemingly aimless hikes always ended at an Italian bakery, where Sam and Stephanie both developed what would become a lifelong passion for cannoli, panettone and zabaglione.

It was a river that flowed two ways. Dave brought Eugene and Maria records from his record store— Italian opera and Italian folk music, Maria Callas and Gigli.

Eugene taught Morley (not Dave) how to grow tomatoes, and how to care for their pear tree.

It was one of those friendships that can only happen between neighbours. A friendship that happened mostly out of doors—mostly in the backyard. A friendship that would never have developed if it wasn't for the children.

Eugene and Maria moved back into the basement apartment the summer Stephanie was fourteen. The move wasn't planned. There was a five-day heat wave at the end of July. On the second night Eugene slept in the basement bedroom because it was cooler down there. Maria joined him the next night.

They moved the television down the night after. There was already a kitchen there, and a bathroom with a tub. They could walk right out into the garden. They had everything they needed.

They moved back upstairs for the winter.

They were both relieved the following May to move back down. They didn't need stairs in their lives any more.

That second autumn, when it was time to move upstairs, they kept putting it off. When they finally went up, they went up reluctantly. Neither of them saying anything about it. Neither of them wanting to admit the house was too big for them. Neither of them wanting to say how heavy they felt when they had to climb stairs.

One afternoon, in the middle of January, Eugene said, "It would be warmer downstairs, you know, closer to the furnace."

They moved back down after dinner. Unknown to Dave they were living a cosy winter hibernation, close to their frozen and preserved garden and, best of all, close to Eugene's wine.

Weeks went by before Dave realized something was different. One afternoon he was looking into the backyard, watching a blue jay at the bird feeder, when he noticed Eugene's lawn chair had been left out all winter. It was while he was staring at the snow-covered chair that he realized he hadn't seen Eugene and Maria for weeks.

It was Morley who pointed out the grapevine hadn't been cut back in the fall as usual.

Dave said, "Maybe they've gone on vacation."

He started to watch the house for signs of life. Every night at nine the lights clicked off abruptly. But it was as if they were on a timer.

"If they had gone away they would have told us," he said to Morley. He went over to check.

They didn't answer the bell. They couldn't hear it from the basement with the television on.

Dave came home.

He was still fretting the next night.

"It's not right," he said. "Something is wrong."

He was worried. He had, after all, told their son he would keep his eye on them. Tony had told him he wanted to get them into a home. Or a seniors' residence. Anywhere there were other people. Anywhere there was a staff to watch them.

Dave went over again the next night. When there was no answer at the front door, he went around the back to look in the windows. He didn't think of looking in the basement until he saw the flickering light of the television. He squatted down and peered through the basement window—and there they were, both of them, asleep in their chairs in front of the TV. Eugene's head was tilted back, his mouth open. Maria's chin was on her chest. For a moment Dave thought they were dead. Then Eugene's leg twitched and Dave said, *Thank you, Jesus,* and went home.

He called on them the next night after supper. By the patio door.

Eugene squinted at him over his glasses. He hadn't shaved for several days. He looked alarmingly old, shuffling back to his chair.

Maria said, "Are you hungry?" But she didn't get up. She didn't even try to put anything on the table.

He worried about them all March, calling every few days, dropping in on weekends.

They always seemed tired. Worn out.

Dear Tony, I am worried about your parents.

He finished the letter, but he didn't mail it.

For two weeks it sat by the cash register at the record store.

On the first Saturday in April, when he woke up, he could tell it was going to be a glorious day. He could tell before he got out of bed by the way the sun was coming through the curtains, by the way the air felt: warm and light on his face. Suddenly, it was spring.

He made coffee. He took it upstairs to bed and read the paper. He heard Sam run downstairs. Heard the door slam. When he finished his coffee, he would go out too. He would take Arthur for a long walk.

When he stepped into the backyard, he took a deep lungful of air. It felt wonderful to be alive. It felt wonderful to be outside without a jacket.

He looked around his yard and smiled. Then he looked next door and almost fell over.

There was Eugene—clutching the top of his ladder as he tried to thread a rope through a pulley he had rigged to the side of his house.

He was leaning out, precariously, reaching farther than he should.

And there at the bottom of the ladder, holding it steady, was Dave's son, Sam.

Dave's first impulse was to drop the dog leash. "Arthur! Stay!" he said. He was about to jog around the fence. He was about to ask how he could help. But he stopped himself.

Eugene had asked Sam to help.

He already had the help he wanted.

Someone who would let *him* be in charge.

Someone who would let *him* climb the ladder.

It took the two of them two hours to uncover the tree and twenty minutes to pull everything else out of the hole.

There wasn't only a fig tree in there. Eugene had also buried his fuchsias, his geraniums, a passion flower vine and a bougainvillea.

Dave went back inside where he couldn't be seen. He stood by the kitchen window watching his son working. He watched him lifting the plants out of the grave, watched him lugging them the length of the backyard. Watched him lining them up in the sun by Eugene's back door.

It was as if spring itself had been buried in Eugene's backyard, as if spring had been lying in that hole waiting for Sam to lift it out and breathe it back to life.

The tree came out of the ground with one fig still clinging to a high branch. They stood it up and packed earth tenderly around the root ball. If only, thought Dave as he watched, if only he could bury an olive grove.

Sam was home for lunch, with a twenty-dollar bill in his pocket.

"I was working for Eugene," he said.

Dave waited for half an hour before he went over to admire their work. Eugene was sitting in his chair smoking.

Maria came out the door.

"Are you hungry?" she asked.

On Monday Dave tore up the letter he had written to
Tony. He wrote a new one on Tuesday night.

Dear Tony,

*There has been a cardinal in your father's back-
yard for several weeks trying to convince us all it
was spring. This weekend it finally had something
worth singing about.*

*Your father and mother were in the backyard for
the first time since October. It has been a long
winter, and as I watched your father working I
thought how he has become like the fig tree that he
loves so much.*

*The winter was difficult—we haven't seen much
of him since Christmas. Like his tree, he spent
much of the winter underground.*

*Last fall you asked if the house might be too
much for Maria and Eugene.*

*An hour after you left, your father came over
and said, "My son wants me in a home. We are not
going to go."*

I didn't mention our talk.

*I don't think you need to worry about them right
now.*

*He got the fig tree up on the weekend. He had a
friend of his over to help out.*

I can see Eugene through the window as I write

this. He is sitting in the yard. He looks tired, but happy.

Dave paused over the next line.

How do you sign a letter like this? To a man you hardly know.

Sincerely, he decided.

Before he signed it, he read over what he had written. Then he looked over at Eugene. He had just lit one of his little cigars. He was waving madly at Maria, trying to get her attention. Maria was at the far end of the garden working on the grapevine, with a pair of pruning shears.

Dave smiled and looked back at the letter in front of him.

I will go and visit them after supper, he added.

They always make me happy.

And I will write again soon.

Love, he wrote.

Love, Dave.

Love Never Ends

There are people you meet when you are a child—
school teachers, coaches, store owners—people whom
you orbit when you are small and without much
gravity, people who influence the way you travel for
the rest of your life. Art Gillespie was such a person
for Dave.

Whenever Dave thinks about Art Gillespie, the
thing he inevitably returns to is a baseball game on a
Sunday afternoon in 1966. Sometimes he starts thinking about that ball game, and it is the ball game that
leads him to Art, rather than the other way around.

Big Narrows Miners versus the Baddeck Junior
All-Stars. Dave playing left field. Art Gillespie
coaching. Kevin Campbell, sliding into third base, is
called out, and Art is exploding off the bench—
storming towards the third base umpire, Scotty
Leblanc. Art, looking for all the world as though he
is going to slug Scotty—which would have had all
sorts of unfortunate repercussions, considering that
Scotty, who owned and operated Scotty Leblanc's
Academy of Music, happened to be teaching Art's
daughter, Milly, the clarinet that spring. Milly was

counting on playing in the Elks' Music Festival in Antigonish, big time.

Scotty almost fainted when he saw Art steaming towards him, his face all red and pushed forward, his fists clenched. It did look bad. Until Art abruptly drew up not six feet from where Scotty was standing. He looked down at his fists and up at Scotty, and then he shook his head as if he was trying to clear it, as if *he* was just as surprised to find himself halfway to third base, and abruptly spun and walked back to the bench without saying a word.

He dropped down beside Dave and said, "You don't have a chocolate bar, do you, Davie?"

It was a most un-Art-like moment. Art never got angry. Art never raised his voice. Dave, his mouth hanging open, his eyes wide with surprise, looked up at his coach and shook his head. "No," he said, "I don't have any chocolate, Art."

Art spat on the ground. "Don't worry. It don't matter."

Art Gillespie, third-generation owner-operator of the Big Narrows Ice Company. Born in March of 1917 on the farm where he spent his boyhood and all his adult life, the farm nestled in the maple bush at the base of Macaulay's hill.

Art Gillespie. Son of Norm, who ran the ice company before Art took it on. Norm, who used to drink with the great pilot Johnny McCurdy.

In fact, eight years before Art was born, Norm used the Big Narrows ice sleigh to drag the Silver Dart—the biplane that made the first powered flight in the British Empire—onto the ice of Baddeck Bay. Norm was, in fact, standing beside Graham Bell the moment the airplane bounced twice and lifted off the ice. He heard the great man mutter "Goddamn" under his breath when the rickety flying machine, or aerodrome as Bell liked to call it, took flight.

Art kept the sleigh in the back of the barn long after his father had passed on, long after they had stopped cutting lake ice, and he would show it to anyone who asked. He would stand by the barn door, tugging on his ears, which were as big and spotty as Portobello mushrooms, enjoying them enjoying it.

Art Gillespie actually flew with John McCurdy when he was a boy. He was five years old. It was 1922. McCurdy took Art up the day Art's father took him and his brother to Baddeck for Bell's funeral.

Art Gillespie, who everyone said could have played ball in the big leagues. He had a tryout with Boston and was offered a contract, but he didn't sign. A month after he came home, they even sent someone, a scout or someone, all the way to The Narrows from Boston to try to talk him into changing his mind.

"It was just a minor-league contract," said Art, when Dave asked him about it that spring Kevin Campbell was called out sliding into third base and Art asked Dave for the chocolate bar.

Dave never saw Art play ball, but he saw him play golf. Art hit the ball long and straight and easy just as you would have thought.

Art and his plaid shirts. Art and his suspenders. Art and his dog.

Art always travelled with a dog at his knees. He had one, a sheltie, who used to chew tobacco. Kept chewing even after Art himself quit.

Art, who moved around town as if he was connected to it by a big elastic band. You couldn't imagine Art leaving The Narrows—he would be snapped back if he went too far. In some ways, he *was* the town. You got the feeling that if *he* left, everyone would have to go.

Art, who started delivering ice when he was thirteen years old, in the days when everyone in town depended on the Gillespies. They had a team of blind horses that pulled the ice wagon in those days—two old pit ponies who knew the route so clean that Art and his brother would jog along beside the wagon working either side of the street as the horses stopped where they were supposed to, without anyone telling them. Norm would ride in the back of the wagon and cut ice—and keep the books. The father had taught his boys a series of hand signals that *his* father had taught him, and as they peeled out of a house, they would either wiggle their hand in the air the way you signal a waiter for a bill (that meant a charge) or they'd swing their whole arm out, like an umpire calling a man safe at home, which meant they had been paid. Twenty-five cents for fifty pounds.

Art, who worked with the horses and could show you a photo of a clipper ship loading ice that his grandfather had cut out of Bras d'Or Lake, bound for Europe. Cape Breton ice, boy. Going to Paris.

Art, who had kept the ice business going. Bought an ice-making machine when refrigeration came and delivered bags of Big Narrows ice cubes as far away as Sydney. He kept harvesting a few hundred pounds of ice out of the lake every January—just because—but he wasn't sentimental about it. He loved the new machine. He would reach into the freezer and pull out a handful of ice cubes, holding them the way a grain farmer might hold a handful of prize seed. He would pop a cube in his mouth, suck on it and then pull it out, saying, "Now that's beautiful ice . . . you put that in a glass of water and it would just shimmer. It's so clear it would disappear."

When he got the ice machine, he bought a storefront on Main Street between the Maple Leaf Restaurant and Judy's Sewing Shop. He opened a laundromat in front and had the ice machine in a room at the back. "Same business," he said. "Just add water." To get to his office (which was in the back, with the ice) you had to walk down a narrow laneway between the restaurant and the laundromat, past the vent for the dryers. Which meant you had to walk through clouds of steam to get to the ice—a fact that pleased Art.

Through the steam to an office that looked like the ticket bureau at the old railroad station—Art's yellowed varnished desk, Art's rubber stamps, a spike for invoices.

Art and his dog. Flannel shirt. Suspenders.

Art, who lived for ice, went to Florida once a year with Betty, his wife. The first time they went was on a bus tour of the southern United States. First stop, Memphis. When Dave asked him about Memphis, all Art said was "The ice was cloudy. They don't know how to make decent ice down there." He didn't like Orlando either: "Shopping malls everywhere." But he liked Cape Canaveral. And he liked the beach. "First thing I did," he said, "was make a snow angel in the sand."

Art.

Art, who made ice. Art, who gave Dave his first summer job. Art, who coached ball.

Art, who had been around long enough to remember the year his family got the first radio in Big Narrows. Nineteen twenty-eight. You had to use earphones to listen. And Art loved to tell the story about how, on account of the earphones, he was the only person in the house, in fact the only person in Big Narrows, to hear the report about the abnormally high tides in the Thames River in London, England. Tides so high they were threatening to overflow and burst the riverbanks. He was eleven years old. They had only owned the radio three days, and he was unaccustomed to the conventions of the medium. He got the Thames River in London, England, muddled with the Thamesville Creek, which ran through The Narrows. He was convinced the entire town was going to be swept away. He insisted on sleeping in the attic for three nights. His mother let him because he was so intense about it, though he wouldn't tell her why. He didn't see the point in getting everyone worked up.

Two years before the Great Flood, as he came to call it, two years before that, when Art was nine years old, Princess Elizabeth was born, also in London. And somehow Art got her muddled up with Elizabeth MacDonnell, the grocer's daughter, who was born the same week. Art was thirteen before he worked out that Elizabeth MacDonnell, the grocer's daughter from Big Narrows, with her brown eyes, her shoulder-length chestnut hair and her winsome smile, wasn't going to be Queen one day.

Art.

Art Gillespie—dead now, a year and a half. No, two years. Two years since he had died.

Whenever Dave thought about that baseball game in 1966 when Kevin Campbell was called out sliding into third base, he would start thinking about Art, about the Great Flood and Elizabeth MacDonnell and about how the kids from The Narrows used to meet the kids from Linquist on Saturday nights and dance on the bridge. Art met Betty at one of those bridge dances. "Walking My Baby Back Home" was playing on a wind-up gramophone.

Art Gillespie gone. Who could believe it?

Dave couldn't. In the days after Art's death Dave would think about these things and be swallowed by a rush of panic. He would never see Art again. It felt like claustrophobia.

He worried because he couldn't remember what colour Art's eyes were. Now wasn't that a stupid thing to get upset about? But there was nothing he could do to stop himself. It upset him.

Art. Goddamn it. Art.

As the months passed Dave's anxiety slowly faded—slowly Art joined that woolly corner of Dave's brain where sorrow and regret hung out. It was a corner Dave tried to avoid, a place he was pushed into from time to time, sometimes by something someone did or said, but just as often by a smell, the wind, the colour of the sky.

The sky was blue and brilliant the autumn afternoon the letter arrived to nudge him back to Art. The letter was from Art's wife, Art's widow, Betty. Oddly Dave had been thinking about Art not an hour before he found the letter in the mailbox and sat on his front steps to read it. On his way home he had walked past a park where a group of children were playing soccer baseball—a game he hadn't thought about for years. His memories of soccer baseball got him thinking of the hours he had spent as a boy bouncing a tennis ball against the brick wall of the Big Narrows' schoolhouse. And once he got to baseball and school there was Art—guaranteed—waiting for him.

So Art was in his mind, or had been anyway, when he arrived home and found the letter and sat on the front steps to read it.

Dear David,

I am writing to thank you for your kind letter which you sent when Art passed on. I feel awful that I haven't replied until now, but at first I didn't feel up to writing and then I kept putting it off. I never seemed to have the time. Or the right time, I guess. But I have as much time as anyone else, so that is no excuse. Please accept my apologies. I hope you understand.

Art always had a fond spot for you, David. I wonder if you know Milly wasn't our only child. Did you know we also had a son? Jack. Jack died in 1955. He had polio. He was nine years old.

You must have been four or five years younger than Jack but I think when Art looked at you he thought of our son. You had the same colouring. I think watching you grow gave him a special pleasure. He always spoke warmly of you.

The day Art learned he had cancer, they told him he would only live three months. He came back from Halifax after the first treatments, and he told me they were wrong. He told me he had three years in him. And he was right. He lived three years and two weeks after we learned he was sick. And I think we did all right. We did the best we could, anyhow.

Remember how we used to go to Florida? We used to have such a grand time. Art was too sick that last April to go. He wasn't getting around much any more. He couldn't even play his guitar. Time was coming when we normally went and he was depressed and one night he said, "I can't go." And I said, "Yes you can." And we did. I paid for four seats so he could lie down across three of them. The first night we stayed in a hotel in Orlando. I drove us to Clearwater the next morning. That was the first time I had ever driven in Florida. Your mother thought I was crazy. She asked me what I was going to do if he died in Florida. I told her I would buy a backpack and have him cremated and bring him home on my back. What was I supposed to do? I wasn't going to sit around The Narrows and wait.

We had a wonderful time. We rented a room on the beach and I put one of those lounge chairs out on our deck so he could see the water and hear the wind in the palms. He was too sick to do anything else, but at least he was warm. At least he was in Florida. And I didn't have to buy the backpack, thank God.

I guess it was while we were in Florida that I really understood he was going to die. I guess that's when I figured there were no emergencies any more. We had moved beyond emergencies. So we might as well keep moving.

We had always talked about when we retired how we would spend some money and go to one of those fancy resorts. The Celtic Lodge or Digby Pines. Some place like that. Two weeks before Art died, he said, "I guess we're never going to do that." And I said, "Yes we are. We are going to spend that money right now. We are going to go somewhere where we can hear loons at night." He said, "I can't even get downstairs. How are we going to do that?" His liver was so swollen he was having trouble sitting up.

I told him in all the years I had been a nurse I had never heard of anyone living longer by sitting in one place and holding their breath. So I bought a blow-up mattress and a line of yellow plastic rope and away we went. We had our forty-eighth anniversary on the lake. They gave us a cottage right next to the dining room. I pulled him to all the meals on that air mattress. I guess we had arrived at a place where we both realized we had to choose between our dignity and doing something we were going to enjoy. So we gave up our dignity. It wasn't hard.

I dragged him down to the water in the morning and we would visit with a nice couple from Saskatchewan and watch their kids swim. I'd pull him back down in the afternoon and we would watch the fishermen come in and see what everyone had caught. Mostly I read to him on the balcony. I would lie beside him and keep him company. When he went to sleep I would work on the mattress. By the end of the week it was pretty much all covered in duct tape. As I said, he died two weeks later. And I am glad we went.

I am sorry you couldn't have been here for the service. The church was full. But the house was some empty that night when I came home. I don't think I will ever get used to that. It doesn't worry

me any more, though I still do funny things sometimes. A couple of months after he died I got up
one morning and set his place for breakfast.
Imagine that! Sometimes I'll be on my way home
and I'll see something and I'll think to myself that
I have to tell Arthur about that. And then I'll
remember, don't be silly.

We used to read to each other at night before we
went to sleep. When he died, we were about a
third of our way through a book of Alistair
MacLeod's stories. The night we buried him I
couldn't settle because the book wasn't finished.
So I went up to Art's grave with a lawn chair and a
flashlight and I took the book and I read to him.
After I was there awhile I heard a rustling, so I
turned off the flashlight. It was deer—three deer
moving from grave to grave eating the flowers.
They would stop by a stone and eat all the cedar
and the greenery and then move on to the next one.
It was the most calming thing I ever saw. Watching
nature come out and seeing how life goes on.
Those three deer picnicking on all those flowers.
I went up there with my chair and my flashlight
and our book every night for a week and a half.

About the third night I found a baggy on his
grave with a letter in it and a picture. It was from
Dunn Lantier. The captain. I picked it up, but I
didn't read it. I guessed Dunn had something he
wanted to say to Art and I figured it was none of
my business. Art was a good friend to so many

people. They would call him and talk things over
with him. I guess other people saw that letter
during the day because before the week was over
the letters started to multiply. Eventually the
groundskeeper put out a box for them. There were
well over fifty. I never read one of them. Though I
did put your letter there. You had so many nice
things to say. I hope you don't mind.

It is funny the things that you miss. Art and I
used to have a little ritual if one of us was frosted
about something and we couldn't sleep. I can't
even remember how it began. I think it was something left over from his childhood. When someone
was peeved up, or things were rough, the other one
would fix a snack. It was always the same snack: a
Cadbury Fruit & Nut bar and two glasses of milk.
And we always ate it in bed. We usually kept a
chocolate bar handy in case of an emergency. Once
or twice when we didn't have one on hand, Art
went out and got one at MacDonnell's and brought
it home and we would have our little picnic.

About three months after he died, I was cleaning behind the bed and I found a chocolate bar
hidden on his side of the headboard. We have a
bed with a dresser and mirrors built in on either
side. There are cubbyholes over the dresser, and I
found the chocolate bar tucked at the back of one
of the cubbyholes. It really tied my buns in a knot.
I wanted to have a picnic right then and there but I
didn't have my picnic partner. I must have cried

over that stupid chocolate bar for three months.

One night I finally decided I either had to eat it before the worms got to it or I had to throw it out. So I decided to have a picnic on my own. I went downstairs and got the tray out and a glass of milk and fixed everything just right and came upstairs. I got into bed and opened up the chocolate bar but there was no chocolate in it. Art had eaten the chocolate and folded up Kleenex and wrapped it all up again with a note. "Sorry. But I was hungry. It was truly delicious. Love you, Art." I had bawled over that chocolate bar for weeks—and I was bawling again and all I had was a handful of Kleenex to wipe my nose with.

I knew I had to do something with it. I got up and wrapped it just the way Art had, and I put on my jacket over my nightie and I went out to the garage and got a garden stake, and I nailed the wrapper to the stake, and then I drove up to the cemetery and I hammered the sucker in right beside his tombstone. I laughed and laughed while I did it.

On the way home I stopped at MacDonnell's and I bought myself a Cadbury Hazelnut bar. I never really liked the Fruit & Nut bar all that much. I didn't favour the raisins, but Art did and I never said anything. So I bought the hazelnut bar and had a hazelnut picnic. I sat in bed eating that bar and laughing so hard there were tears coming down my face.

I put up a tree this Christmas. I couldn't do that last year. When I pulled out the decorations I found a Christmas stocking he had packed for me. He must have packed it the spring before he died. I guess he knew he wasn't going to make it to Christmas. There was a bag of marshmallows that were as hard as rocks, and a necklace, and a Cadbury Fruit & Nut bar and fifty American dollars. He always gave me American money at Christmas. I used to use it in Florida to take him out to dinner. I still have that fifty-dollar bill.

You have been more than patient to read this old woman's ramblings. I just wanted to thank you for writing. I would love to see you the next time you come home.

His eyes were blue.

Yours sincerely,
Betty Gillespie

Dave sat on the steps for a good half an hour after he had finished reading the letter. He didn't exactly cry but he must have looked messed up. Three different neighbours walked by during the half-hour he was sitting there—they all waved but none of them came up the walk to talk. Not even Jim Scoffield, who hesitated and then kept walking. "I'll see you later," he said.

Dave didn't show the letter to Morley right away. He handed it to her that night when they were in bed, reading. Morley said, "What's this?"

When she finished it and handed it back to him, she had tears in her eyes. Dave was ready for that. He smiled, and took the letter and put it in the drawer of his bedside table. Then he pulled something out of the drawer.

"Here," he said. "I thought you might be hungry."

He was holding a chocolate bar. Cadbury Fruit & Nut.

How to Listen to *The Vinyl Cafe* on Your Computer

- Go to the website: **www.cbc.ca/vinylcafe**.
- Click on the "Listen to CBC Radio" icon located on the right side of the web page. This will direct you to a map of Canada and a list of Canadian cities.
- *The Vinyl Cafe* is broadcast on both Saturdays and Sundays (in Canada).

Saturdays

On Saturdays, *The Vinyl Cafe* is broadcast at 10:00 A.M. Eastern Standard Time on CBC Radio Two. Listen by clicking the RADIO TWO icon. (Note: 10:00 A.M. Eastern Standard Time is the same as −5 UTC or Coordinated Universal Time.*)

Sundays

On Sundays you can listen to CBC Radio One. The same *Vinyl Cafe* program is broadcast in five different time zones as follows. Click on the city you want to listen to at the appropriate time.

Halifax   12:00 P.M. Atlantic Standard Time (UTC −4)
Toronto   12:00 P.M. Eastern Standard Time (UTC −5)
Winnipeg   12:00 P.M. Central Standard Time (UTC −6)
Calgary   12:00 P.M. Mountain Standard Time (UTC −7)
Vancouver 12:00 P.M. Pacific Standard Time (UTC −8)

Enjoy, and thanks for listening.

* UTC is Coordinated Universal Time. It is the same as Zulu time or GMT (Greenwich Mean Time). A helpful web page that will show you the UTC where you live is **www.timeanddate.com/worldclock/**.